White Coral
A Chase Gordon Tropical Thriller
Douglas Pratt

MANTA
PRESS

MANTA PRESS

For Ashlee

1

"Another round?" Jay asked, despite still nursing the Jack and Coke in his glass. The ice had melted, but he'd only finished half of it.

"You're babysitting me?" I questioned him, pointing at his glass as evidence of my accusation.

His face twisted as if I was being ridiculous. "Not at all," he howled, turning up the watered-down cocktail to drain the glass.

"Fine," I retorted before waving at Glen, the bartender at Pat's.

"Need another, Chase?" Glen asked as he swiped the empty glasses from in front of us.

"Yeah, another round," I told him. My eyes locked with Jay's in a silent game of chicken. "Give us two shots of Patrón."

Jay didn't flinch, but I suspected he wanted to.

It was a little puerile of me. In fact, it was paramount to bullying. He was babysitting me.

Jay was a detective in the Palm County Sheriff's Department, but he was also one of the deadliest people I knew. Jay Delp could pick a cherry off a bar from two football fields away with a rifle. He and I served in the Marines together, and if anyone was going to have my back, it would be this man.

Of course, there was no need for his marksmanship at the moment. No, Jay's concern was because my drinking had gotten somewhat excessive. Which, if I was willing to be self-aware enough, should have been a worry. After all, Jay was never one to shy away from a weekend of whiskey and women. That might have even been the cause for a couple of his divorces.

However, I didn't agree with him.

I knew I was in a funk. I'd been there for the last few months.

Normally, I sail back into West Palm to work a few weeks to put enough money together to take my forty-foot Tartan sailboat, *Carina*, back out to the islands. When I'm cruising, I live cheap enough that whatever I sock away can last for months.

However, I'd been in port for almost three months. At first, I was helping Missy get the Manta Club up and running after a major renovation. Weeks turned into months, and I had no set plans to get back out.

It's one of those quandaries of the soul. The best thing I could do would be to untie the dock lines, point the bow anywhere the water is clear, and raise the sails. Unfortunately, I wasn't motivated to do it.

Deep down, I knew what I should do. Jay had suggested taking a weekend to run over to Bimini for some diving, but I hadn't committed to anything.

Instead, I'm slinging drinks behind the bar until we close. After that, I either find my way to Pat's or some other late-night dive, or I find my way to Missy's bed. Technically, her office or my bed, since her waste-of-space husband is often in her bed.

Glen brought another Jack and Coke for Jay and a Rum Runner for me. He set down two shot glasses with a semi-clear liquid in them. Salt covered the rims of both glasses with a bright green lime wedge hanging on the side.

Without batting an eye, Jay pulled the lime off and hoisted the glass up. We clinked glasses in a silent toast and swallowed the tequila.

"Damn!" Jay whistled as he slammed the glass down.

"Another?" Glen asked hopefully.

I could see Jay wave him off. "If I don't slow my pace, I'll end up married again," he quipped.

Glen retrieved the empty glasses and moved down the bar.

"Chase!" a falsetto voice shouted over the bar.

"Abby," I greeted the newest cocktail server at the Manta.

The girl was in nursing school on her daddy's dime. When we met, she told me she was twenty-five and working on the ten-year graduation plan. She pulled her blond hair back into a ponytail and donned a pair of red glasses instead of her contacts. She was still wearing her cocktail uniform–a black dress that drew attention to her breasts and hips.

"What are we drinking?" she asked as she slipped onto the stool next to me.

"Rum," I announced.

She waved at Glen, signaling her desire for a matching drink. After Abby placed her order, she leaned across me, pressing her breasts against my arm, and introduced herself to Jay.

"I'm Abby," she bubbled. Her smile spread across her face. "I work with Chase."

"Jay," he told her, offering his hand. "You look like you just got off work."

"Yeah," she sighed. "I had to work with Hunter. He's not nearly as good as Chase is."

"Behind the bar?" Jay joked.

"Probably anywhere," she jabbed back with a provocative glance at me.

I felt Jay's eyes cut to me, curious.

"Let's do a shot," Abby squealed. "Glen, three Fireballs."

"I'm good," Jay insisted. Abby narrowed her eyes at him before leaning toward me, whispering, "He's a pussy!"

I laughed. "No, we just did tequila shots."

Her infectious grin spread. "Fine. Three tequilas, Glen."

Jay started, "I didn't mea..."

"Too late," she bellowed as Glen brought three more shots over.

Jay sighed and downed the tequila, immediately squeezing the lime between his teeth.

"Woo!" Abby cried.

Someone distracted her, and she spun around to talk to a guy I recognized from the area.

"Nice girl," Jay commented.

I cocked my head to look at him.

"Seems she really likes Chase," he continued.

"Why wouldn't she?" I exclaimed. "I'm delightful."

"Hmm," he mused. "What about Missy?"

My brow furrowed. "What about her?" I asked. "She's at home with her family."

"Come on, Flash. Who are you kidding?"

I rolled my eyes. "She's kinda young," I stated in defense, gesturing toward Abby.

"Yeah," Jay muttered with some skepticism. "Like ten years. That's not that big a gap."

"Depends on the age," I remarked.

"I suppose. She's what? Twenty-four? Twenty-five?" he asked.

"Twenty-five."

"It's not the same as those tag chasers we saw in our twenties. The age difference isn't as big a deal as you get older. Unless the girl's a teenager. Even nineteen is stupid young. Most don't do more than starfish anyhow. Who needs that?"

I nodded in agreement.

"Besides, what do you talk about with a 19-year-old?"

"Led Zeppelin?"

"As if," he coughed.

"You need to get back out there," he added. "Let's go gear up. Doesn't bug season start soon?"

"No. Lobster season's still a couple of months away," I reminded him.

"Whatever," he scoffed. "I have a badge. We can tell Fish and Wildlife it's part of an investigation."

I grinned. "How much time do you have?"

"Hell, I got a few weeks," he remarked. "How much trouble could we get in over a couple of weeks?"

I considered it for a few seconds. "Alright, I'll look at the weather," I agreed. "If it's favorable, we can cross next week."

"Good," he smirked. "Maybe we can bring along Selena Gomez there."

My right eyebrow arched. "You just commented that she wasn't too young?" I questioned.

He shrugged. "Yeah, but that's my MO. Not yours."

My eyes rolled again. "I'm entitled to sow some wild oats," I pointed out.

"Your whole life is 'wild oats,'" he remarked. "You live on a boat and snorkel while the rest of the world is clocking in and out of the doldrums of life. But you are usually more sensible about women than I am."

"Right," I argued. "The most stable relationship I've had in years is with my married boss. That's sensible."

"Comparatively," he pointed out.

"Comparatively what?" Abby interjected, popping back into our conversation.

"Jay was just telling me I lived wild and fancy free," I told her.

"Doesn't he?" she squealed. "He lives on a boat. Like, he can just step off the side if he wants to swim."

Jay smirked again. "Life is grand, Flash," he prodded.

"Who's Flash?" Abby asked.

"That's his call sign," Jay explained. "From the Corps."

"Oh, y'all were Marines together?" she asked.

I nodded.

"What does it mean?" she questioned. "Flash?"

Jay explained, "Everyone gets a call sign. Sometimes it's a big joke. Other times it's just an easy mnemonic. You ever hear of Flash Gordon?"

She shook her head. Jay cut his eyes at me.

"*Flash Gordon* was an old movie from the eighties. Super cheesy, but killer soundtrack. You've heard of Queen?"

"Yeah," Abby acknowledged. "From the movie."

"Right," Jay replied, dragging the syllable out with his trademark Mississippi drawl.

"Wanna do another shot?" she asked.

Jay shook his head. "No, I gotta work in the morning."

"Chase?"

I stole a look at Jay. "Sure."

Jay's head shook slowly as he stood. "You can get home, right?" he asked, reaching for his wallet.

"I got it," I assured him. "My treat."

He slapped me on my shoulder. "Make sure you get back safely."

"Dude, I live three blocks away," I reminded him. "If I could find the hotel in Dubai, I certainly can make it to my boat."

"Nice to meet you, Abby," he offered.

She bounced past me and wrapped her arms around him. "You should really stay sometime," she urged.

"Another time," he promised.

"Hey, Jay," she said with a giggle. "We need to make Flash take us out on his boat."

He lifted the right corner of his mouth in a wry smile as he cocked his head. "Did you hear that, Flash?"

"Great," I retorted. "She can come to the Bahamas with us."

His eyes narrowed as Abby jumped up and down. "Can I really? When are you going?"

"We don't have it ironed out yet," Jay interjected.

"Jay, you could bring that girl from Phi Cum Alotta," I suggested in jest. "Make it a foursome."

He offered a subtle gesture of surrender. "I have to go. Night, y'all."

He weaved through the bar toward the door. The Budweiser clock on the wall read 2:23.

Abby slid another shot of tequila in front of me. She must have ordered it while I was talking to Jay.

"Come on, Flash," she urged. "Let's have some fun."

She winked at me from behind the red-framed glasses. I grabbed the lime and slammed the shot back. When she slammed the glass on the top of the bar, she leaned into me, pressing her chest against me. Her face moved close to mine, and her breath was hot. The din of the bar melted away as she smiled at me.

"Do you wanna kiss me?" she breathed.

"Definitely," I admitted.

"Are we really going to go sailing?"

You know those moments when you know the right answer. Those that cause the least drama. The ones that make perfect sense. When every fiber of your being knows the right answer. That moment. When you have the cheat sheet and everything, but you answer wrong anyway.

In case you missed it, that was this moment. I knew better. Still, I kissed her.

I tasted tequila and juice on her lips. For several seconds, the rest of the bar seemed to vanish. Not that it was the most amazing kiss. She had excellent technique, but it wasn't in my top five or anything. No, it was as if I was standing across the room watching someone else. I wanted to tap myself on the shoulder and point out all the reasons everything about this was probably a mistake.

Yet, it didn't stop me.

Until the hair on the back of my neck stood on end.

I pulled back from her. She had both hands on my cheeks, but I looked past her.

To the two men that just entered Pat's.

Built like wrestlers, the two Latino men wore expensive suits with the chrome of a gun under each of their lapels.

They locked eyes with me and walked toward me.

"Uh, Abby, we should go," I informed her.

"Oh, yeah," she breathed.

"Mr. Gordon," the larger man grunted as he stepped in front of us. "We would like to have a word."

The one talking had a small cross tattooed below his left earlobe and two teardrops on his cheek. The other man snarled, flashing a glint from the gold teeth in his mouth.

They'd closed the gap between us, leaving a finite amount of space between me, Abby, and the two of them.

I shook my head. "I don't think so," I informed them.

"It wasn't a request," Tattoo growled.

"Everything okay here?" Glen asked over my shoulder.

Gold Tooth scowled at him. "Get out of here," he snapped.

"Uh, Chase?" Abby's voice shook.

"It's okay, Abby," I assured her. Looking back at Tattoo, I cocked my head and replied, "See, those aren't proper manners. I don't respond to demands."

"You want trouble?" Gold Tooth asked.

I turned to Abby and pursed my lips. "I'm sorry, Abby."

"Sorry..." she began before I shoved her past the bar stools behind her. Abby fell back and landed on her butt.

Before she landed, I swept the half-full hurricane glass I'd been drinking. The Rum Runner and rim of the glass smashed into Gold Tooth's face. Shards of glass cut his cheek, and I brought my knee up hard into his groin.

Tattoo reached under his coat for the gun, but by closing the surrounding quarters, he left me able to lean into him. My entire body shoved against him, pinning his hand between our torsos. He reacted as I hoped, pushing back. My head came back. My forehead landed on the bridge of his nose. The blow stunned him, sending him back a step.

My right hand shot up and caught him in the throat before I followed up with a punch to Gold Tooth's jaw. The embedded glass sliced my knuckles as I drove several pieces deeper.

My hand grabbed Gold Tooth's lapel, jerking him forward. My left snatched the gun from under his jacket and aimed it at Tattoo, who had recovered enough to get his own weapon free of the holster.

He just didn't have time to aim it.

I was holding a Desert Eagle .44 caliber. The barrel leveled at Tattoo's chest. If I pulled the trigger at this range, the bullet would punch a hole through his sternum, explode his heart, and leave a gaping hole in his back as it exited.

Tattoo was smart enough to know that. He let his grip on the Smith & Wesson .45 loosen, letting it hang on his index finger.

I reached over and took the .45 before glancing at Abby.

"You okay, Abby?" I asked.

"Oh. My. God. That was insane," she screamed.

"Chase, I can call the cops," Glen informed me in a somewhat dumbfounded tone.

I smiled at Tattoo. Gold Tooth was holding his bleeding face.

"What do you want?" I demanded.

"We're supposed to take you to Mr. Moreno," Tattoo told me.

"Seriously?" I asked. "Where's Scar...I mean, Esteban?"

Tattoo shrugged.

"Where's Julio?"

"At Padrino's," Tattoo answered.

I glanced at Glen. "Did anything get broken?"

"Besides them?" he questioned.

I nodded.

"Just the glass."

I turned back to Tattoo. "How much cash do you have?"

He shrugged. "*No sé*. I don't know. Couple of hundred."

"Give it to him," I demanded.

Tattoo reached in his pocket and pulled out a wad of bills. He handed it over the bar to Glen, who took it warily.

"Take Jaws here to the doctor," I ordered Tattoo. "Next time, I suggest you lead with Moreno's name."

Tattoo nodded, looking at both guns in my hand.

"I'll keep them."

"What do I tell Mr. Moreno?"

"It's almost three in the morning. Whatever he wants can wait until tomorrow."

"*Por favor...*"

I interjected, "You can explain to him how the evening went. I think he'll understand my annoyance."

Tattoo turned with some dejection and motioned for Gold Tooth to follow.

When they left, the rest of the crowd at Pat's stared at me.

"Sorry, Glen," I apologized again. He shrugged, holding the stack of bills with a smile.

"Damn, Chase," Abby exclaimed, pressing against me. "Can we leave now?"

2

The odor of stale beer and mildew hung in the air. I found Abby curled next to me in her full-size bed. Streams of light cast beams from the ragged blinds, illuminating the millions of dust particles floating through the room. Abby's small studio apartment was six blocks west of Pat's outside the area I called the beach zone, where the condos and hotels provided access to the white sands.

The hike back to *Carina* would have been closer to Pat's, but Abby seemed intent on coming home. At the time, it didn't matter to me. I rolled my feet to the floor, letting my bare toes dig into the brown shaggy carpet.

The effects of the tequila passed while I was asleep. While hangovers didn't bother me, a little coffee would go a long way right now. My feet padded around the room as I picked up my clothes.

I collected the two guns I pulled off Moreno's henchmen last night. They didn't need to be lying around Abby's place. It was a fair bet that either weapon had been used in some crime.

Abby had at least fifteen reusable grocery bags hanging on the cabinet in her kitchen. I stuffed both weapons into one with a unicorn hurdling a rainbow. After winding it into a tight ball, I stuck it under my arm.

It was almost half past nine. Even when I closed the bar, I didn't sleep this late.

The residue of sex, sweat, and tequila covered me. I was pretty sure I still had a bit of Gold Tooth's blood on me, too. When I peeked in the bathroom, I decided to head back to the Tilly Marina for a shower.

Quietly, I slipped out of Abby's place and headed to the street. It took me half an hour to walk back to the Tilly Inn. *Carina* remained berthed at the marina behind the hotel.

I aimed for the sidewalk that skirted the building and led to the water. A black Suburban pulled up on the curb beside me. I turned as the passenger window lowered. Tattoo sat behind the steering wheel.

"Mr. Gordon," he called in a much more civilized tone than he had used last night.

I stared at him, waiting for a request.

"*Señor* Moreno would like to meet with you. If you are available."

"See, that's so much nicer," I commented.

Tattoo nodded. "I can drive you to see him," he remarked.

I weighed the option. Julio Moreno wasn't the guy one refused twice. Not without some consequences. The man headed most of the drug trafficking in Florida, and he stretched that territory toward Texas. Telling him "No" wasn't a healthy option.

At least, this time Tattoo exhibited some manners. Also, he seemed to be alone in the Suburban.

"I could use a shower," I told the man.

"*Señor* Moreno won't mind," he assured me, confirming that refusal this time would not be acceptable.

The unicorn bag was still under my arm, meaning I had quick access to a weapon if this was more than a taxi service. However, I didn't think Moreno would let Tattoo do anything to me. Of course, I didn't discount the fact he wanted some payback for last night. It just felt like an acceptable risk.

I climbed into the back seat. The vehicle had a "new car" smell, but I guessed someone just detailed it regularly.

Tattoo put it in gear and pulled away from the curb.

"I hope there aren't any hard feelings," I commented.

Tattoo shook his head in a slow motion, as if an invisible force demanded it. "*No señor.*"

"How's your friend?" I asked.

His eyes cut up to the rear view mirror, judging my sincerity.

"He needed some stitches," he muttered.

"Sorry," I offered.

He grunted back. Likely, Julio Moreno didn't appreciate their approach and subsequent failure. Tattoo received a reprimand. Otherwise, I doubted he'd be so complacent.

He continued south into Miami. It was obvious where he was taking me. Julio Moreno held court in a Cuban restaurant called Padrino's. The place catered mostly to the local neighborhood, but the authenticity and quality brought outsiders to the restaurant. It was situated halfway down a block filled with empty buildings. Most of the neighborhood was run-down shops, closed convenience stores, and a few dilapidated houses.

I wondered how much of the real estate along this stretch was controlled by Moreno. If you wanted to keep people out of your business, keeping the neighborhood empty was a start. Unfortunately, he couldn't do much about the DEA, who had almost twenty-four-hour surveillance on Padrino's.

Tattoo pulled up in front of the restaurant, letting me out like he was my personal chauffeur. As I closed the door, I noted the service van a block south. The engine was running, no doubt to keep the AC cold. I tried to ignore it as I went inside.

The restaurant wasn't open yet, but a young high school-age girl stood at the hostess stand. She watched me walk inside, apparently recognizing my description. Without offering me a seat, she asked, "Mr. Gordon?"

I nodded.

"Follow me," she ordered as she turned to walk to the back corner.

A partition wall papered with beach scenery separated the back table from the rest of the dining room. Julio Moreno sat at that table. His back would be toward the door. He didn't like to be overheard, and the partition, along with facing away, was a defense to any eaves-dropping devices the government attempted to use.

Moreno sat with a fresh espresso and the remains of a pastry. He glanced up as the hostess approached.

"Chase," Moreno greeted me. "Please have a seat."

The other six seats at the table were empty. It was an unusual sight. Every time I'd been in Padrino's, the table was never empty. Usually Scar, Moreno's right-hand man, was with him. His name wasn't actually Scar. It was a moniker I gave him before I knew his name was Esteban Velasquez. The mnemonic was based on the jagged scar across his face. While I only called him by his name, the nickname rattled around in my head.

I pulled out a chair next to Moreno.

"Carlita," Moreno called to the hostess. "Will you get Mr. Gordon an espresso?"

I nodded my appreciation. Coffee had still eluded me this morning.

After dropping the unicorn bag on the table, I scooted it toward the drug czar.

"Interesting bag," he quipped as he unfolded the top to peer inside.

"Thought your boys might want them back," I informed him.

"Hmm," he mused. "You certainly ruined their evening."

"Perhaps they should have used a bit less aggression," I pointed out.

Moreno's head bobbed. "Yes, my apologies," he offered. "My instructions should have been clearer."

"Yes," I agreed. "If they'd have led with your name, it might not have caused a scene."

Carlita returned with a tiny cup filled with espresso. She offered me a spoon and sugar, but I waved her off.

Moreno cocked his head in deference when he told me, "Thank you, Chase. Jorge said you chose not to involve the police last night."

"It almost got out of hand," I informed him.

He nodded as if to say the discussion was over.

"What can I do for you, Julio?" I asked, sipping the espresso.

Moreno reached into the inside pocket of his jacket and pulled out a stack of bills, the banding read $25,000. He plopped the money in front of me.

My eyes cut from the bundle of bills to Moreno. "What is this?" I asked.

"I need a favor," Moreno explained.

"People don't pay for favors." I explained, pushing the money back. "I don't work for you. There is no point in the future where I plan to work for you."

"Mr. Gordon," he spoke in a harsher tone intended to intimidate me.

This wasn't new ground. Moreno made a couple of offers in the past that I flatly refused. However, he'd also lent his expertise on a few things, meaning, at least in his mind, I owed him a little. However, a man like Julio Moreno will attempt to subvert any debt into ownership. I wasn't about to find myself sworn to the drug lord. I needed to balance our relationship.

He cleared his throat. "May I ask you a favor, Chase?"

I leaned forward. "Ask away."

Moreno's head turned from side to side, ensuring the restaurant was empty and no stray ears were tuned on us. Finally he began, "I need to find Esteban."

Shocked, I straightened up in my chair. "What happened to him?"

"This is very"–he paused as he seemed to search for the right word–"sensitive."

"I'll keep it quiet," I promised.

"There is a family in Cuba. Competition, if you understand my meaning."

I nodded.

"Two members of this family were killed yesterday."

"By Esteban?" I asked.

Moreno responded, "It seems so. Juan Moralez, the father, has reached out with a threat. He wants Esteban to pay or else."

"Or else what?"

"He declares a war," the drug lord answered.

"And you plan to offer your man to prevent this?" I asked.

Moreno shook his head. "Not unless I have to. There could be a lot of blood, though."

"Did you send him to do this?" The question was moot. It wasn't likely that Moreno would admit to contracting a murder. He might trust me with some secrets, but nothing that would have consequences for him.

He shook his head, and I didn't know if I could trust him.

"Why not send Tattoo, er...Jorge?"

"For Esteban?" Moreno retorted with a wry smile

He was correct. Esteban Velasquez was a deadly enforcer. The guys last night were amateurish, and someone like Scar would have killed them on the spot. Whereas I displayed a ton of restraint.

"And you think I could do it?"

"You certainly have the abilities," Moreno acknowledged. "But also, Esteban respects you."

I chuckled. "Respects me," I repeated. "That just means he would have to try a little harder to kill me."

Moreno nodded. "*Verdad*. But a man like you would stand a better chance."

I stared at the man for several seconds, trying to decipher what he really wanted. Did he expect me to confront Scar? Only one of us walks away? I'd gone up against Scar before, but he misjudged me at the time. It wouldn't be a mistake he'd make again. Now, though, his hackles were already up.

"What happens when I find him?" I asked.

"I need to know if he did this," Moreno explained. "After that, I have to decide if I go to war for him."

The answer was odd. If I were in his shoes, it would be easy. Scar was his closest associate. Maybe not as close as Jay and I were. At least, the dynamic wasn't exact. Still, I'd go to war before I offered him up to my enemy.

In truth, I might battle it out for Scar, too. The man was a raging sociopath, but I respected him on some strange levels.

"I will not kill him," I stated flatly.

Moreno stared at me.

"When was the last time you spoke to him?" I asked.

"Three days ago," he responded. "On Wednesday. He didn't show up Thursday. I sent Jorge to find him, but he wasn't at home."

"Alright," I conceded. "I'll look for him, but if it gets weird, I'm out."

Moreno's mouth twisted into a half smile. "Will you need anything?" he asked, nudging the money toward me.

"His address," I responded, pushing the money back. "Where were the two men killed?"

"Up north. Naples," Moreno told me, jotting down Scar's address on a napkin.

I swallowed the rest of my espresso. "Okay, Julio. If I can find him, I'll let you know."

"I'll have Jorge pick you up out front."

"No, ask Carlita to call me a cab," I told him.

I pushed to my feet.

"Have a great day, Julio," I suggested.

The silver-haired man dismissed me with a nod. I walked past Carlita, who was already on the phone.

"The taxi will pick you up out front," she informed me when she hung up. I didn't see Moreno signal her, and she hadn't been close enough to overhear us. It left me wondering how she anticipated the cab.

Without offering it much thought, I stepped out into the sunshine. The Miami heat immediately started drawing perspiration to my skin. It didn't matter to me. I would take being drenched in my sweat and devoured by mosquitoes over snow and ice.

A dark blue sedan pulled up to the curb. A middle-aged, lanky white man climbed out of the passenger seat.

"Get in the car," he demanded.

"I don't think so," I retorted.

The man flashed a badge at me. I read Drug Enforcement Agency on the top.

"Get in the car, or I can arrest you."

I lifted my hands in surrender and walked to the back seat. It was a bluff, and I knew it. He could detain me, even arrest me, but there was no evidence to make anything stick. Still, sometimes it's good to hear what people want to know. The man slammed the door and slid back into the passenger's seat.

The driver turned to stare at me through wire-rimmed glasses, saying, "Chase Gordon, what are you doing with Julio Moreno?"

"Agent Kohl, right?" I replied. "I wish I could say it was nice to see you."

3

"Are you arresting me for having coffee?" I demanded.

The DEA agent leaned his elbow on the shoulder rest and adjusted his glasses, pulling a few strands of gray hair under the temple tips resting on his ears. "Call me curious," Van Kohl commented. "If I see a piranha swimming with some goldfish, I'd like to know what's going on."

"Are you calling me the piranha or the goldfish?" I questioned.

He grunted and drove away from the curb.

"I was waiting on a cab," I pointed out.

"Not anymore," he denounced. "You're going to answer some questions first."

I leaned back against the seat. A faint hint of tuna hung in the car. The agents lived out of this vehicle, eating most of their meals in the front seats.

Kohl and I crossed paths before. His career hinged on arresting Julio Moreno. Unfortunately, he'd gained no headway. While I didn't hinder his investigation, I wasn't the willing witness he hoped. His bravado never intimidated me. It was something he wasn't used to, and that rubbed him the wrong way.

I stared out the window with my arms crossed. Graffiti adorned the walls of the declining buildings. After a few minutes, Kohl pulled to the side of the street.

"Let's talk, Gordon," he demanded.

My eyes studied him. He seemed to have gotten grayer around the ears since I saw him last.

"What are you doing with Julio Moreno?" he asked.

My arms folded across my chest, and I said nothing.

The taller agent in the passenger seat blurted, "Smart ass. Do you know what you are getting into?"

My head tilted down so I could glare up at Kohl. "New guy?" I asked.

"Jackson's not new," Kohl spat.

I shrugged. "This seems like a repeat of the last time we met," I reminded the agent. "One would think you'd learn."

"Gordon, there's a turf war brewing," Kohl told me. "Moreno's man, Velasquez, is AWOL, and you just show up. Looks like Moreno might have hired new muscle."

I chuckled. The fact Kohl only considered Scar to be "muscle" was part of why he'd never jail Moreno.

"You think it's funny!" Jackson shouted.

"Jackson, why don't you just play with the radio or something?" I scolded in an even tone.

The middle-aged agent fumed, his eyes searing through me.

"Are you arresting me, Kohl?" I directed my question to the driver.

"I might," he threatened with little conviction.

"You won't," I responded. "If you had anything worthwhile, you'd act on it."

"Fine, Gordon," he relented. "We need your help. Something is happening, and we need the inside scoop."

"So you thought picking me up in front of Moreno's business was going to convince me to face off against a man like him?"

Kohl stayed silent.

I bobbed my head. "What makes you think Velasquez is missing?" I asked.

"He hasn't been around in days. That doesn't happen."

"Perceptive," I jabbed. "He could be on vacation."

Jackson snorted. "I've been on them for two years, and the man's always here."

I shrugged. "You think someone killed him?" I questioned. "You mentioned a turf war. Who the hell is bigger than Julio Moreno?"

Kohl stared at me.

"You don't know anything, do you?" he remarked.

"I told you that already," I pointed out.

"No you didn't," Jackson interjected.

"Oh, right. Well, I meant to."

Kohl let out a sigh. "Why were you there?" he prodded again.

"Coffee."

"What do you know about Naples?" Jackson asked before Kohl could cut through him with his eyes.

"The city in Italy or the one in Florida? It doesn't matter, because the answer is little about both."

"Stay out of this, Gordon," Kohl warned.

"I don't even know what I'm supposed to avoid," I told him.

"Get out," he ordered.

"I had a cab coming to the restaurant," I informed him.

"You can catch one here," he told me.

I opened the door. "Can I borrow your phone?"

As I stepped onto the sidewalk, Kohl noted, "That's right, you don't have a phone. Too busy sailing the world."

"Yeah," I confirmed. "Can I borrow yours to call a cab?"

"No," he announced, pulling away as the rear door swung closed.

My head shook at the man's gall. He must be a whiz at fostering witnesses.

The sun reflected off the concrete. My hand shielded my eyes as I peered up and down the street. Kohl left me six or seven blocks away from Padrino's. Most people would consider this stretch of neighborhood rougher than even the area around the restaurant. The difference was the lack of protection afforded it by Moreno and the Andrade cartel.

Kohl might have abandoned me on principle. Our last encounter left him in the lurch with those above him at the DEA. It was also possible it was a power play with Jackson. He needed to prove his ruthlessness to his partner. It's also possible the man is just an asshole trying to show me who is in control.

Whatever, it didn't affect me. Well, it annoyed me as I hiked toward a more trafficked street. If I'd gone back to Padrino's, I could get Carlita to call another cab. Even catch a ride with Jorge. Of course, Julio might question why the DEA picked me up, but those questions didn't bother me. I don't believe Moreno was worried about any testimony I could give Kohl. If he was, the only man he had to go against me was taking a sabbatical.

I hoped it was as simple as a voluntary break. The idea of Scar cut down or dumped in the swamp somewhere didn't sit well with me.

Not because I liked the man. Respect has little to do with affection.

No, it wasn't that. If something made a man like Scar vulnerable, it could affect all of us.

Kohl left me in a wasteland. Only a miracle would send a cab down the street in this area. It was still early enough in the day that the only people on the street were the homeless and drifters finding alleys and doorways to sleep. They milled up and down the street like extras in a western film. The main characters hadn't arrived on set yet, and only the nameless were in the scene. Later this afternoon, the neighborhood would fill with a more dangerous crowd. It was the same in every major city.

Some seemed lost in their own world, walking through life in a dream. They talked to themselves or shouted at unseen people. Others were fully aware. Their eyes followed me as I passed each one of them. The glare moved from the last set of eyes to the next.

I considered my options. If Scar was alive, and to consider otherwise seemed pointless at the moment, where would he hide? There was a better question. Why would he hide? I didn't want to believe Moreno would kill him unless he betrayed the drug lord. However, I didn't grasp the intricacies of the cartel. Would a gang war worry Moreno enough?

The only places I could start were Scar's home and Naples, Florida. Kohl assumed Scar was missing, too. He called him AWOL, which was vague.

Moreno had given me Scar's address in Miami–a condo in Coconut Grove. I wasn't as familiar with Miami as I was with West Palm, which said little since I could navigate exactly four blocks around the Tilly Inn. Anywhere else left me lost.

It took forty-five minutes to hike toward Highway 1. Traffic picked up, and I stuck my thumb out.

Hitchhiking is a brutal business. Worse than dating. Thousands of cars whiz past you, ignoring the request.

I stood for two minutes when a white Taurus pulled over. Amazed, I ran toward the brake lights before they could change their mind.

There were two people in the front seat–both looked like men.

"Thanks, guys," I offered as I slid into the back seat. "I'm heading to West Palm."

Without a word, the driver shifted into drive and pulled into traffic. Both men were Latino, and as soon as the car began moving, I got an uneasy vibe.

The passenger twisted to stare at me with the barrel of a Smith & Wesson .38 lying across the shoulder rest. He grinned a crooked, sinister smile, flashing two chipped teeth.

"Listen, guys," I began. "I can get out here."

The driver responded by pressing the accelerator down. With a whine from the engine, the car sped up. The driver weaved through the cars as the needle on the speedometer wiggled past sixty miles per hour.

"You work for Moreno?" the chipped-tooth man asked.

I studied him carefully. The dark pupils didn't waver, and he savored the moment.

"Moreno who?" I responded.

He jerked around and shoved the gun toward me. "Don't fuck with me!" he snapped, sending spittle over me.

"You know, I just want to go home and take a shower," I muttered with feigned exhaustion. "What do you want?"

"We saw you leave Moreno's," he hissed. "We saw the DEA. Who do you work for?"

"Neither of them," I offered. "It's a big misunderstanding."

"Who are you?" he demanded, pushing the gun toward me.

I swallowed, but didn't answer.

"I'll kill you," he rasped. His voice was cracking with frustration.

"In your car?" I asked. "It's a bitch to clean that up."

He rattled something in Spanish to the driver. Too fast for me to decipher, thanks to the ineffectual teachings of my middle school Spanish teacher.

"Who are you?" I asked.

"None of your damn business!" he shouted. "I'm asking the questions."

"Do you work for Juan Moralez?"

The man's eyes widened. "I knew it. You're Moreno's man."

He turned his head for a split second to deliver another round of Spanish. I swept my left hand up, rotating the elbow like the hand of a clock. The barrel of the .38 pushed away from me as my right hand shot up into Chipped Tooth's face with several rapid strikes.

Everything slowed when the gun fired. It was an instant that dragged out.

The gunshot deafened me when it went off.

I knew that the driver didn't slump forward.

Instead, the bullet knocked his head into the driver's window. Or it would have if it hadn't exited the other side of his skull and shattered the window.

The dead man's grip released the steering wheel, and either the motion of his body or the sudden loss of control spun the wheel to the left. The Taurus veered into the next lane at over sixty miles an hour. It careened into the front end of a Volkswagen Jetta, bouncing over the hood like it was a tall curb.

My fist was still in mid-swing to deliver another punch to Chipped Tooth's face. The blow never landed. I threw myself into the floorboard, wedging myself between the back seat and the two front seats.

The Taurus collided with the concrete barrier separating the northbound and southbound lanes of traffic. Momentum shoved me into the front seat, but the tight quarters kept me from moving much. Metal crunched as glass rained down on me. The smell of talcum powder filled my nose.

I tried to move. The front seats seemed to have shifted back during impact. As I pushed up, I got my left elbow under me and reached up with my right. The windows on both sides had shattered. Both airbags deployed, but Chipped Tooth was sitting almost backwards. When the bag exploded, the impact broke his neck.

I crawled out the rear window and flopped to the ground. My knees pushed me up, and I crawled away from the wreck.

I used my hand to pull myself up as my equilibrium caught up to my body. The impact crumpled the Taurus like a crushed aluminum beer can. The Jetta wasn't in much better shape. Everything from the windshield to the bumper was crushed.

In the distance, I heard sirens wailing. This was going to be difficult to explain. By the time the cops sifted through the evidence, it would be obvious that Chipped Tooth shot the driver. Until then, this mess would wrap me up like a tangled net.

4

"You just left?" Jay asked. He sat at the corner of the Manta Club's bar. His hand spun the nearly empty beer bottle as he scraped the label off.

"I wasn't driving," I pointed out.

"It's still illegal," Jay reminded me. "How d'you get home?"

"Walked to a Holiday Inn and called a cab."

He shook his head as he took a sip of beer.

"Did you look up the killings in Naples?" I asked him.

"Yeah. Naples PD found two men shot in a home invasion. Lisandro Salcido and Renaldo Bernal. According to the report, it was a shootout in a house on Bottlebrush Lane. It looked like someone barged in with guns blazing. Both of the men were armed. It looks like they shot back, but crime scene and ballistics reports haven't verified that yet."

"Sounds like a fun time," I remarked as I moved to the other side of the bar to check on the lawyer with the gin and tonic.

It was the late afternoon, which meant the bar wasn't busy. Too late for lunch, too early for dinner. A few stragglers would wander through, but for the next hour, it would be quiet.

"You know Kohl's got a hard-on for you," he reminded me.

I shrugged.

"Seriously, leave Moreno alone here," Jay advised.

"I know," I agreed. "I should, but something is bothering me. It seems out of character for Scar."

"To kill a couple of guys?" Jay questioned. "That seems in character for the man."

"Sure, he'd do it for Moreno, but this is something else."

Jay shook his head in disbelief. "If the nice drug lord is telling you the truth."

"I can always bail if it gets hairy."

"Hairy?" Jay repeated. "What do you call the two dead hitters on the highway? Not to mention the poor girl in the ICU."

The driver of the Jetta was a twenty-three-year-old nursing student on her way to class. Now she was hanging on in the hospital. I tried not to think about her, but when Jay mentioned it, my heart sank. If she died, it would be my fault. I didn't have to fight the two men. If I'd waited for a better moment, she'd have made it to school safe and sound.

I wasn't about to tell Jay, but it was the thrill. After fighting Jorge and Gold Tooth the night before, I felt a rush I enjoyed. When Chipped Tooth pointed the gun at me, elation washed over me. I knew it was going to get bloody. It was a welcome jolt from the last few months I'd wallowed through.

There wasn't even a thought to wait a few minutes. The man would not shoot me in the car unless he had no choice. I had plenty of time for the right moment. I just didn't wait.

Now, this nursing student was in critical condition.

"How well do you know Velasquez?" Jay asked.

"It's not like we hang out," I explained. "But he's a soldier, too. We have a mutual respect."

"Hmm," Jay mused. "Don't go thinking he wouldn't put a bullet between your eyes if Julio Moreno told him to."

"I won't disagree."

Jay's eyes shifted over my shoulder for a split second, and my head rotated to see Abby come through the door.

"Your new friend's here," he joked.

I rolled my eyes back at him.

"Seriously, it's smart of you. The kids' menu is always cheaper."

"Shut up," I scoffed.

He guffawed as I walked around the bar. Gin and Tonic waved me off as he typed on his phone. Abby stashed her purse under the cash register.

"Hey," I called, rather poetically.

"You snuck out," she replied with a slight grin. "I was hoping for another round this morning."

"I had to take care of something," I told her.

"Those guys from last night?" she asked.

I nodded.

"That was amazing, by the way," she admired. "You were so fast."

"They were too cocky," I pointed out.

"It scared the hell out of me," she gushed.

"I'm sorry about that," I offered.

"Hell, it was the hottest thing ever."

My lips pursed as I stared at her.

"Listen, Chase," she almost whispered. "I'm not looking for anything serious."

"Oh!"

"Hell no," she reiterated. "Besides, everyone knows you and...uh...Missy have a thing."

"It's not like that," I tried to say.

She grinned. "It was fun, though. I still want a trip on your boat."

I nodded, somewhat dismayed.

Abby squeezed my hand. "I'm running to the ladies' room before anyone shows up."

As she skipped away, I walked back to Jay.

"You planning a romantic date at Chuck E. Cheese?" he quipped.

"No, she doesn't want anything serious," I explained.

He broke into laughter. "You're disappointed," he noted.

"I am not," I refuted. "I wasn't looking for a relationship with her, either."

He continued to laugh. "No, but you wanted to be the one to decide that."

My eyes narrowed as he chuckled.

"Shit," he whispered. "You have company."

I turned to see two large, nearly identical goons standing in the doorway. The two Latino men towered over the room at well over six feet. Both appeared to spend a massive amount of time building muscle, and if someone told me they were linebackers for the Dolphins, I'd believe them.

"Recognize them?" he asked me.

I shook my head. Jay pulled his phone out as I walked around the bar.

"Afternoon," I greeted them. "Get you a drink?"

The goon squad walked down the three steps leading from the lobby of the Tilly Inn. When they sat on the bar stools, the wood squeaked under the weight.

"You Gordon?" one asked me.

I pegged him as the senior of the two. The hierarchy of these things is clear if unstated. It's rare for a pair to be equal. There's always something that elevates one over the other. Sometimes it's simply dominance. Few people can handle an egalitarian dynamic.

"You are?"

"You killed a couple of our friends," he growled.

My hand wrapped around a paring knife I had been using to cut up limes. The blade was only two and a half inches, but the edge sliced through the rind like it was butter. I'd find myself hard-pressed to take out both giants, but if either tried to go for a weapon or reach across the bar, I would make them regret it.

"I don't know what you're talking about," I responded, staying a foot out of his reach.

He ignored my answer. Instead, he leaned across the bar with a sneer on his lips. "We want to know where Velasquez is," he demanded.

"Everything alright, here?" Jay asked, strolling around the bar. He dropped his badge on the bar, visible to the two behemoths. When he sat on the stool three seats down, he rested his M45 gun on the top of the bar.

"No problem, officer," the brute announced.

"Are you ordering?" Jay questioned.

Both men took turns staring at each of us before the first replied, "No, I don't think so."

As each of the three-hundred-pound men stood up, the stools creaked as if sighing with relief. Goon One gave me a hard stare before turning to leave—a silent warning he'd be back.

"Seems like you have a big bullseye slapped on your back," Jay commented after the two vanished into the lobby.

I pulled another cold beer from the fridge and popped the top before setting it in front of him. "If I don't find Scar, I might end up with a convention here."

"Want me to wait around here tonight?" Jay offered. "In case the Boulder Twins return."

"I'll be fine," I told him.

"Those weren't Moreno's guys, were they?" he asked as he put the beer to his lips.

"I don't think so. The two in the car asked if I was working for Moreno. If these two were their friends, it stands to reason they belong to Moralez, too."

"Sounded like they blame you for the wreck," he pointed out.

I stared up at the door, considering what Jay said. Somehow my visit to Padrino's labeled me, and it might not be smart to remain too stationary. It made me wonder how much trouble Scar was into. I thought Moreno displayed some exaggeration about the so-called "war." However, the troops were forming up on the other side, and now they assumed I was involved.

"You want some food?" I asked Jay.

"No, I'll drink another beer in case your friends return."

I nodded and moved around to Gin and Tonic, who tapped his glass while he talked on the phone.

Jay's presence left me assured. However, he needed to remain uninvolved. The sheriff might frown on one of his detectives becoming embroiled in a drug war.

Two more guests came through the door as Abby returned. She directed them to a table near the window.

The evening ran past. Jay drank two more beers before slipping out the door as the bar filled up. By eight, the dinner rush passed, and Abby was cleaning up the tables.

The goon squad never made a return, but as we closed up, I palmed the paring knife, just in case. When I made it back to the boat, I'd pull the M45 from the compartment I added in the v-berth. Most of the countries I cruise to don't have the same gun laws we do in America. It seemed best to ensure I had a weapon stored somewhere overlooked during a cursory inspection by any local officials.

"Wanna go get a beer?" Abby asked when she finished cleaning her area.

"I think Pat's needs a break from me," I retorted.

She shrugged and gave me a wink. "Next time," she advised, tossing the wet rag into the bin for laundry. "You have much more to do?"

I shook my head. "Twenty minutes or so. Have a great night."

"See you next time," she told me, smiling as she carried the bag of towels to housekeeping.

The doors shut behind her, and I found the drone of ESPN to be my only company. It seemed prudent to lock the doors leading to the lobby while I counted my money. I considered heading over to Jay's house. Even getting a room upstairs for the night might be smart. If those two boarded *Carina* while I was asleep, it might result in some trouble.

In the end, I just wanted to crash into my berth. I could sleep with my M45 under my pillow. After years of military sleep patterns, I became a light sleeper. The slightest shift in the boat would wake me up. I'd be awake and in a firing position before they opened the companionway door. At that point, anyone coming through the doors was the target at the end of a shooting gallery.

Once I cut the lights out, I took a long path toward the marina. There were a few lights on some trawlers, and as I passed a couple of slips, I could see the television flashing in the ports.

Carina seemed peaceful–exactly as I'd left her before my shift. Nonetheless, I stepped on carefully with the knife, ready to attack.

Once below deck, I breathed a sigh of relief. I secured the companionway with an anti-theft bar I'd designed. It wouldn't stymie anyone attempting to break through, but it should slow them down. There would be plenty of time to get out of bed and shoot whoever tried to come through unannounced.

It seemed smart to wake early, untying the dock lines, and relocate to Bimini or Grand Bahama until this Moreno thing blew over. I didn't owe anybody, certainly not Moreno or Scar.

Somehow, that option seemed ludicrous. Tomorrow, I'd go to Naples. The idea of diving into the lion's den energized me.

Once settled, I cracked a cold Red Stripe from my fridge and collapsed on the settee. Three beers later, I couldn't sleep. Still, I turned out the lights and sipped the cold beer.

5

Instead of borrowing the marina's courtesy car, I had Charles, the hotel's valet, give me a lift to the car rental about six blocks away.

Once, before I joined the Corps, I drove a beat-up Ford Ranger. It was the only vehicle I ever owned, besides *Carina*. After two summers of tossing hay bales and mucking barns, I earned enough to buy the truck. It offered my sixteen-year-old self an escape from the screaming and yelling that seemed ever present in my house. I bounced over gravel roads and two-lane highways looking for anywhere to go that wasn't my house.

I drove it until my eighteenth birthday, when I shipped off to Parris Island. It sat in my mother's backyard until I got out of basic training. After that, I paid to store it in whatever port I shipped out from. After several years, the poor thing looked neglected. Despite the nostalgic yearning to hang on to it, I eventually let it go for exactly what I'd paid for it.

Since then, I have had little use for a car. When I got out of the service, my plan was to spend all my time on a boat. A truck seemed pointless. Now, most of my life is on the water.

The Tilly Marina had a courtesy car for transient cruisers to borrow, so it easily accommodated any quick trips to the store. However, Naples was on the other side of the state. It seemed prudent to get a rental for a few days.

Missy wasn't in her office yet, so I left her a note explaining that I'd be away for a few days. She'd need to get Hunter to cover my shifts.

I figured when I got back, she'd have an earful for me. If Jay knew where I was going, he might offer a few words as well. It wouldn't take a lot for him to figure it out. He'd already given me the details on the shooting in Naples.

The dealer put me in a topaz Nissan Versa. After yesterday, I opted for the extra insurance. Not that the insurance helps if I'm plowed into a concrete barrier, but in the hopes I survived, it would alleviate any troubles down the road.

I tossed a small backpack into the backseat and pointed the front of the little Versa west on I-75. The ride along 75 takes one on a two-hour tour of the most anesthetized roadway through South Florida. Most of the view is trees in the Big Cypress National Preserve. While the two-lane roads through the wilderness make for some scenic drives, the freeway plowed through it, allowing only a passing glance at eighty miles per hour. However, this trip wasn't recreational, and efficiency counted more than scenery.

Bottlebrush Lane wasn't in the type of neighborhood one would expect for a shootout to occur. Statistically, it was reasonable to assume some of the residents of these homes undertook a fair amount of criminal activity, but I realized those crimes would largely be white collar. Large homes with three to four thousand square feet of living space lined both sides of the streets. Most were new construction, and I guessed close to seven figures, if not more. Wrought-iron gates guarded over half of the drives, suggesting a degree of privacy maintained and insisted by the owners. Who wants a neighbor popping over for a cup of sugar nowadays?

The address Jay gave me led me to a long concrete drive gleaming the sun back at me. There was no gate, but wooden pallets stood on end and tied together with yellow tape acted as a barrier. The yard had been mowed; however, there was a distinction between this yard and the rest. Most of the neighboring homes had soft carpets of Bermuda trimmed exactly four inches from the ground. This house had a variety of grass types mixing in with the Bermuda. Several shoots of crabgrass and plantain cropped up across the yard.

There didn't seem to be any police presence at the moment. Despite that fact, I didn't think entering the house was worth the considerable risk.

While the cops weren't around, the neighbors were out in force. Several joggers chugged past me, huffing, as if proving the point they were working hard. Two women worked in their yards, offering the impression their immaculate landscapes were due solely because of their efforts. I pulled up to one where a woman was milling around her bushes. Her house sat just two doors south and across the street from the house where the shooting occurred.

As a general rule, if appearances matter to the person, they notice what others do. The gossip who judges everyone will know all the juicy details. Growing up in the South taught us all to know who has all the goods.

The woman was in her forties and quite attractive. Adorned in tight leggings and a tank top, she pruned the straggling stems of a red hibiscus. Her head turned to watch me as I pulled up in front of her house.

I'm not a small guy, but despite my six-foot, two-inch stature, I think I have an amiable enough face to come across as nonthreatening. Still, I worry about startling a woman alone in her front yard.

She rose to her feet, holding the shears she'd been using at the ready. Her grip was useless. In order to do any damage, she'd need to turn them with the point out. The way she held them now was only useful if she were attacking Norman Bates style. It was utterly defenseless.

It didn't seem prudent to point that out.

The diamond ring on her finger was large enough to reflect sunlight across the bay if needed. She wasn't planning to work too hard out here, otherwise she'd have left it inside rather than risk dirt packing between the stone and the fitting. Even her wedding band had clear stones along the center.

"Good morning," I greeted her with a smile. "I'm wondering if you have a second to answer some questions?"

"What is it about?" she asked warily. Her eyes narrowed as she examined me. I didn't fit in this neighborhood. Even my car, despite being somewhat new, was a poor fit here.

I glanced over my shoulder at the house across the street. Enough of a hint to stir the gossip in her, while not actually prodding her.

"Are you with the police?" she asked, folding her arms. She wasn't at ease yet with me, but her grip on the shears and her defensive stance were both relaxed now.

"No, ma'am," I answered.

"We don't have time for tourism," she scolded me. "Two people died."

"Sorry," I offered, raising both hands as if surrendering. "I'm not a tourist. I work with the insurance company."

She looked me over, scrutinizing my attire. "Do insurance agents dress like that?" she asked, waving her hand toward my shorts and sandals

"It's Florida," I explained with a congenial smile. "I'm on my way to the golf course. This was just a stop I needed to make."

She nodded, as if that made perfect sense. Work was something she expected others to do, but not something she took part in. It wouldn't be a surprise if she didn't expect the golf course to be part of most people's workday. Likely, her banker husband spent a couple of hours a week hitting balls with clients.

"Is there a lot of damage?" Curiosity and gossip usually win over common sense.

"A fair amount," I told her.

"Is the owner coming back?" she asked.

"The owner?"

She nodded again. "She's probably not the owner. Just lives there, I'd guess."

"Sorry," I apologized. "Corporate hasn't sent me all the paperwork yet. Was the owner not one of the victims?"

"No, it was two men. The girl that lives there is in her twenties."

"Interesting," I noted. "How long has she lived there?"

"Just a couple of months," the woman explained.

"Odd," I commented. "There was no woman listed on my paperwork. How long have you lived here?"

"Six years," she responded. "That house hasn't had the same person in it for over six months at a time. The first couple bought it right after we moved in. Think they were from Atlanta or Alabama. I don't know. Declared bankruptcy. Some guy bought it a year later and flipped it. Spent a ton of money fixing it up. He sold it for less than he put into it."

"Seems stupid," I remarked.

"My husband thinks that was a tax deal."

I nodded as if I understood how that might work.

She continued, "Then it was the singer. She stayed three months before she disappeared. Too good to talk to anyone around here. Since then, it's been a few months at a time. This girl seemed nice enough. She'd have her boyfriend over a lot, but most of the time, it was just her."

"Who were the guys killed?" I asked.

"I heard they were her friends. Probably selling her drugs or something."

"Were you home when it happened?" I asked.

"Yeah," she told me. "I didn't hear it happen, though."

"Scary. I hope you're being safe."

"My husband says the cops'll keep it locked down for a while. He says there shouldn't be anything to worry about."

"Hopefully, the police will keep an eye out for any trouble," I assured her. "Do you know the young woman's name that lives there?"

She shook her head. "I never talked to her. Just waved when she was in the front yard."

"Can you describe her?"

"She was Hispanic... er... Latina... I don't know. Something. Dark hair. Beautiful girl."

"You never saw the men that were killed?"

She shook her head again.

"Thank you," I told her.

"What insurance company were you with?" she questioned as I walked away.

"Florida Fidelity," I lied.

She seemed satisfied. "Enjoy your golf," she shouted after me as I opened my car door.

I waved back before getting inside.

My next stop was the local library. I needed to search for a few things on the internet.

Much like the truck, I also gave up a cell phone. Actually, being in the Marines helped that. I didn't take one with me to Parris Island. After I left the island, I realized how nice it was to keep my family away. Their drama often had a way of bleeding into my life, no matter what I did. By ditching the phone and heading to Afghanistan, I controlled how often we talked–which was rarely.

Once I got out of the Corps, I found there wasn't a lot of service on the sea. I'd call my sister every few months when I was back at the dock, and she'd leave a message at the Manta Club for me.

All of that left me a little behind on technology. I was not a complete troglodyte, but everything took me a bit longer to do.

The silver-haired librarian smiled as I came to the desk.

"I'm looking for some information about a house," I told her. "I'd like to find the owner's name."

"You'd need to go to the property records for that," she explained.

"Where is that?"

"Let me get you on a computer," she advised. "We have people researching that type of thing all the time."

I sighed with relief. Once she put me in front of the screen and told me the web address, it only took a few minutes to navigate the website for the county property assessor. It was easier for me to find the map and zoom into the street rather than search by the address.

Clicking the print icon, I waited as the printer whirred and buzzed. The property data sheet stated the owner was Carl Oxenwise. The county delivered his tax bill to an address on Captiva Island, just an hour and a half north of Naples.

I folded the paper and thanked the librarian before heading to my car. My stomach rumbled, so I pulled over at a little seafood shack overlooking the Gulf.

6

Carl Oxenwise's home on Captiva was close to the same size as the one he owned on Bottlebrush Lane. The two-story house stood on a side street in the interior of Captiva Island. From an outsider's perspective, the street resembled exactly the one in Naples. If I hadn't performed a double-check, I'd have sworn the same people were working in these yards, right down to the forty-something blonde pruning her hibiscus.

The Versa slid to a stop in Oxenwise's driveway, and I wrestled to pull my frame out of the little car. It was a subtle reminder that if I ever invested in another vehicle, it needed to be off the ground a bit. The engine popped as it cooled.

A gentle breeze rustled the leaves on the roses, hibiscuses, and azaleas planted around the meticulously manicured yard. A little sign said Wilson and Sons maintained the landscape. The edging along the driveway was so uniform, I'd have sworn Wilson and Sons must use a ruler to get it exact. It was a vast difference to the home in Naples. This one was Oxenwise's personal home, and like the women with the hibiscuses, some self-worth came from its maintenance.

A walkway made of flat river rocks stretched to the house. I walked along the stone path to the front porch. The smooth stone gleamed as if recently washed, leaving the mortar between each piece fresh and white.

When I stepped up onto the porch, I froze. The hairs on my neck straightened.

The front door was ajar. Just a crack. In fact, I hadn't noticed it from the street. Up close, though, two teeth marks left by a pry bar were clearly visible. The impression dug into the wood door just level with the dead bolt, revealing the bare splintered wood beneath the white paint.

I backed away from the door, looked around the neighborhood, and when I saw no one paid me any attention, I walked back to the car. I had stashed my M45 in my backpack, and now I pulled it out. With a quick push of the release, I verified the clip was full, and I slipped the .45 under my waistband at the small of my back. The bottom of my shirt covered the weapon.

The cold metal against my skin reassured me as I walked back up the stone path to the front door. My toe nudged the bottom of the door. It swung open with a slight creak. I stole another glance around the neighborhood. Hibiscus woman was still trimming the same three branches, but she seemed to pay no attention to anything else.

"Hello," I whispered, just loud enough to claim I'd said anything. There was no point in announcing myself, but I didn't want to bust in on Carl, either.

The house exuded an empty aura. Everything was still. I stepped into the door. From somewhere, a motor buzzing softly broke the silence. It sounded like a refrigerator, but there was a rattle, as if the compressor was touching the side.

Shiny white tile covered the foyer. A small cherry table ran under a large mirror in a gold embossed frame. Just past the entryway, there was a stairwell arching up the wall. A cherry banister that matched the table climbed the steps with ornately carved spindles holding it up. Each carving was a different version of the same slender mermaid–her hands and fin in varied positions as she lifted the rail.

My right hand rested on the grip of the .45 in my waistband, ready to draw it if a need arose. As I stepped past the stairs, I found myself in a den, filled with large windows that offered natural light throughout the room. A large brown Chesterfield sofa sat in the center of the room. Two matching chairs faced the couch.

As I scanned the room, I found it in disarray. Someone had pulled every drawer in the room out–the contents thrown on the floor. The bookshelves built into one wall showed signs of a thorough search. Several volumes lay scattered where someone pulled them from the shelves.

I reassured myself with the cold steel in my hand as I moved with deliberate steps through the room. Oxenwise's book collection consisted of former bestsellers with a few reprinted classics bound in leather with gold lettering. His tastes leaned toward thriller fiction with authors like Child, Thacker, and Brown. Several broken knick-knacks lay on the floor as if whoever searched the place knocked them over carelessly during the search.

The next room was a stark white kitchen, complete with double ovens, two deep sinks, and a food prep island with a six-burner gas range. The room was in a similar condition to the den. Drawers of utensils were dumped on the floor. The inserts from nearly every cabinet had the contents spilled across the floor. Even the pantry wasn't spared, having been torn apart. Containers of sugar and flour sat upended–their contents spilled into two white mounds on the counter.

Was someone searching for something or leaving a message?

Touching nothing, I moved from room to room. Most of the spaces appeared the same way, as if someone were looking for something. In the bathroom, two pieces of the toilet lid lay broken where someone had tossed it to the floor. A small nick in the tile showed where the lid struck the ground.

Was it Scar? Or was Oxenwise the target, not the two men?

After a walk-through, I found no one at home. Nothing seemed to be taken. All the furniture and decor appeared to be there, except for the few pieces broken during the careless search. It wasn't a burglary–too many valuable trinkets were still there. The house felt void of all life. There was a sense of violation in the structure, although it may only have been a perception I placed on it.

Once I'd been through every room, a sigh of relief escaped me when I found no one, alive or dead, in the house. A sense of dread about what might be behind the next door filled me as I reached each closed door.

I thought the less time I spent in a crime scene, the better off I'd be. Nothing I saw offered me a clue to the whereabouts of Carl Oxenwise or the girl from the other house. Certainly nothing pointed toward Scar's location.

My retreat was as careful as my entry. The reminder in my head went off like an alarm, "Touch nothing."

When I stepped out of the front door, the sunlight felt like a spotlight alerting the neighborhood to me. Yet, no one looked up. Hibiscus woman wasn't in her yard anymore. She'd put in her time. Maybe now her schedule demanded margaritas by the pool.

Once I was in the rental car and backing up into the street, I felt relaxed–that sensation of relief when one has done the forbidden, gotten away with it, and can breathe easy. It was somewhat reminiscent of an adrenaline rush. I don't know how to define it, but it seemed rewarding.

For a few seconds.

Until I saw the Lexus pull off the curb a block behind me. It could have been a coincidence. It was the middle of the afternoon, and the neighborhood was busy. The Lexus could belong to any house. It was the perfect model for the residents here. I rationalized it before I worried. It could be a soccer mom taking her players to practice or running to the store for a pork tenderloin for dinner.

The Versa moved along in traffic, and the Lexus remained exactly six cars behind me. Now it was looking like less of a coincidence. Soccer moms aren't so fastidious about their driving.

The way I saw it, I had two choices: lose them or use them. Losing them would be easy. It just required

breaking a few traffic laws to get ahead of them. While the
Lexus no doubt had a faster engine, I trusted the Versa's
smaller size might elude the SUV in heavier traffic.

But I didn't necessarily want to lose them. A Lexus
might fit into the upper-middle class neighborhood we
were in, but it wasn't the vehicle of choice for the police.
That meant it could be Scar, some of Moralez's men,
or even Oxenwise himself. The only way to find out
was to confront them or follow them. Since I hadn't
eaten since breakfast, I didn't want to spend all afternoon
trailing them. It would take too much effort to maintain
an inconspicuous distance, especially if they were already
expecting it.

That left confrontation, which, if I'm being honest, was
all I wanted anyway.

Despite that desire, I wanted a level of control. That
came from preparation or location. Sometimes both.
Today, I was leaning toward location. Someplace public
enough to prevent open warfare, but where people often
kept to themselves.

I weaved along the roads toward the beach. Traffic
thickened as I reached the coastal road. Blue water
stretched out to the west, bouncing rays from the
afternoon sun off the waves. Along the busier stretches
of the road, vacationers filed across the street. A line
of swimsuits, wagons, and folding chairs crossed at each
intersection. The passage seemed to time itself with every
light change. I pulled into a small lot opposite the Gulf. As
I got out, I watched from the corner of my eye as the Lexus
passed me. The SUV only had a driver in it, but with the

bright light gleaming off the water, I couldn't make out his features.

For a brief second, I considered pulling back out and heading the other direction. That seemed like an opportunity lost. There was only one guy. With the crowd on the beach, it would be tough to come straight at me.

Once I tucked the M45 in my shorts, I crossed the street, noting the Lexus parked a block away. It would take a minute or two for the driver to catch up to me. I could meander, but I thought he should work for it. Several hundred yards south, a line of beach shacks offered chair rentals, umbrellas, beer, and snacks.

When one is being tailed, it's tough to avoid turning to look for the tail. Are they closing in? Are they still there? If you check, you give away the fact you know. Even if it seems impossible for them not to know, don't confirm it for them. It ruins the element of surprise. I suppose the reverse is also true, which is a powerful reason I didn't want to follow them.

So, my brain told me I couldn't risk a look. Instead, I trudged through the sand, dragging my sandaled feet. When I passed the first hut, I took advantage of what I hoped was a moment when I was out of sight. It was an obvious ploy. Whoever was behind me would be an idiot for not suspecting something. Still, I played it out.

The shacks were all built on short stilts that lifted them off the sand about two feet. The raised height prevented flooding with extremely high tides or storm surges.

I dropped to the sand and rolled between the legs until I was under the structure. On my belly, I waited until I saw shoes not designed for the beach–rattlesnake skin boots. I'd seen similar ones in the past, and I belly crawled out the back.

I took two steps around to face Scar, who stood with his arms crossed.

"What are you doing here?" he demanded. He motioned to the ground where I'd just emerged. "This is stupid."

I considered responding by offering a traditional sarcastic comment when the two goons from the bar last night stepped around the corner. Behind me, another figure closed us into the space between the shacks.

Goon One held a Glock 9 mm in his hand, shielding it from the people milling along the beach. The other two carried Glocks as well.

"Velasquez," Goon One growled. He glanced at me. "We have unfinished business, too," he remarked.

7

"Gordon, you're a fucking idiot," Scar hissed at me.

I stared at the enforcer. He kept his eyes locked on me. My toes were acutely aware of the loose sand in my sandals. The two shacks on either side of us blocked most of the sea breeze, and despite the shadow they cast, the air was stifling. Scar's eyes burned, and I sensed his intent to make a move. His gaze was gauging my intent.

As a general rule, I like fights I can win. Most of the ones I've faced are winnable. Unfortunately, I don't always have the luxury of picking the fights. I inhaled, tasting the microscopic bits of sand mixed with the salt air.

The girl in the Jetta flashed through my mind.

Don't be rash, I reminded myself. The M45 remained pressed against the small of my back. However, the three armed men could gun me down before I ever got it free. Scar would attack, somehow. When that happened, I could use the opening. Hopefully.

"I'm not the one starting a war here," I snapped back. "This is on you."

"Shut up," Goon One ordered. "You're going to take a ride with us."

"They obviously followed you," he pointed out.

"The only person following me was you," I replied. "Besides, if you'd just flag me down instead of being all stalky, we could have avoided this.

"Shut up!" Goon One repeated, shaking the Glock in his hand to remind us he was in charge.

The other two exchanged glances. Scar ignored the giant's demands. Instead, he scowled at me. "What are you doing here?" he asked again. The behemoth's eyes flared. With his size, people rarely ignored him when he talked. He possessed an intimidation factor that came with sheer size. Armed, he expected a level of respect that we weren't showing him.

"Dammit!" Goon One shouted, lowering his weapon in frustration.

Scar was a blur as he struck Goon One in the throat. He followed with a punch that landed in his sternum, knocking him back and leaving the behemoth sucking for air. The other two gunmen seemed frozen in shock. Goon One outweighed and out-muscled Scar by nearly a hundred pounds.

The shock and awe of Scar's attack left me the opening I needed. With far less speed than Scar, I caught the third guy's wrist, twisting and dragging him to the ground. He slammed into the sand with my knee landing on his wrist. The impact wasn't hard. However, the angle of his hand made the blow traumatic. A bone-crunching crack left his right hand useless, and I looked up in time to see Scar's hand flash toward Goon Two. Something silver flared through the air, and my brain took a full second to realize it was a blade. The point drove into the man's arm, and Scar slammed his forearm down on the man's hand, jarring the 9 mm from his grip.

Goon One recovered. He lowered his shoulder as he prepared to charge Scar when the enforcer raised Goon Two's Glock level with the first man's head. The thug's eyes narrowed as he realized he was staring down the barrel of a 9 mm. The fact a ruthless killer brandished the weapon seemed to register as his pupils widened. My hand came up, holding the third man's Glock in my grip. The sights pointed toward the injured second brute.

The giants stared at Scar before looking my way. Goon One dropped his gun into the sand. I couldn't see Scar's face, but I felt the tension between the five of us.

"Shooting them on a public beach might cause us more trouble than we need," I pointed out.

Scar grumbled something in Spanish.

"I don't speak Spanish," I reminded him.

"Fine, what do we do with them?" he asked.

"Unless you want to march them out of here at gunpoint, we should send them running."

"They'll be back," he stated.

"Next time you can kill them," I advised.

Both of the goons shifted their gaze at me. Even from behind Scar, I thought he might have smiled at that.

"Go," he ordered the two.

"Take this one," I added, as I stood up. "He's gonna need a cast."

The man I'd taken down pushed himself up with his good arm. He muttered something in Spanish I assumed was more curse than blessing.

Goon One glared at us.

"*¡Vete!*" Scar ordered.

The three men shuffled through the sand. Scar and I lowered our guns, concealing them before some passerby sounded an alarm. He stepped around the corner and watched the three men move down the beach. I scooped up Goon One's Glock, slipping it under my shirt. The other gun I shoved into my pocket. With three guns, the waistband on my shorts was dragging off my hips.

Scar turned back to me. "Did *Señor* Moreno send you?" he asked.

"Yeah," I responded. "In a manner of speaking. He offered me a lot of money to come after you, but I refused it."

The man stared at me. "Why are you here then?" he questioned.

"Since I left him, several people have tried to come after me. All of them looking for you."

He cocked his head with curiosity.

I added, "I thought you might need some help."

Scar folded his arms again. A bewildered look crossed his face.

"That seems stupid," he commented.

I shrugged. "Maybe I get bored," I explained.

"The last time I saw you was after your friend died," he commented.

"Well, you helped me out," I pointed out. "It seemed like I might owe you."

The Cuban shook his head. "You are a strange one," he remarked.

"Those guys are going to be coming back," I pointed out.

"Not yet."

I smiled. "Good. I'm hungry. Let's go find something to eat."

We stopped at Scar's Lexus to deposit the extra guns. He wanted to toss them in the nearest trash can, but I didn't like the idea of three Glocks finding their way into some kids' hands. Despite his protests, he agreed to stash the weapons.

A few blocks north, we found a local place called the Mucky Duck. The hostess put us on the patio. I ordered the fish and chips while Scar seemed content with a Milagro tequila on the rocks.

"What did Mr. Moreno say?" he prodded as he sipped his drink.

"He told me about the two guys in Naples. Apparently, he's fielding calls from Juan Moralez about a breach. He said something like a war was coming. He might have used the word 'brewing.'"

Scar sneered at me.

"He offered me a stack of bills to find you."

The enforcer snorted.

"You find it funny?" I asked.

"I have an immense amount of respect for *Señor* Moreno; however, he believes he can solve all problems with bullets or money," he explained. "He finds you...What's the word? Confusing. Most people would do something for him because they wanted him to owe them. You don't."

I shrugged. "I'm an enigma."

He stared at me.

I continued, "I, of course, refused his money. But the DEA picked me up. Agent Kohl warned me of a turf war. No sooner had I gotten away from the feds, two of Moralez's men tried to kidnap me. I figured if they were coming after me, I might as well find out what the hullabaloo is all about."

His right eyebrow lifted as he took a sip of Milagro.

"What is Moralez after?" I asked. "Were those two guys close to him or something?"

Scar shook his head.

"He just has it out for you?"

"He's looking for 250 of cocaine," he told me.

"Two hundred and fifty kilos?" I stammered. "That's a lot of powder. What's that worth?"

"In Miami, about five million dollars."

"Damn, that's a lot."

The waitress appeared with my plate of fish and chips. Scar ordered another tequila.

"How does one lose five million dollars' worth of cocaine?" I questioned, after swallowing a bite.

"Someone stole it," he explained. "Picked it up at the drop before Moralez could get it."

It made little sense for Scar to take that much cocaine unless he was doing it for Moreno. In which case, it would be an opening salvo of war. Based on my conversation with Moreno yesterday, he was trying to avoid a war.

I studied Scar's face. He was formidable, but he always struck me as loyal. He'd take a bullet for Julio Moreno. It made little sense for him to go behind his back like this.

"Moralez thinks you stole it?" I asked him.

"He may assume I'm involved, but he knows who stole it."

I waited as he sipped on his tequila. Finally, he continued, "One of his former runners. Victor Berríos."

I shook my head, trying to grasp the details. "His guy steals the stuff, and he suspects you're in on it. I guess the two guys in Naples were looking for Berríos?"

My brow furrowed before Scar could respond. "Wait," I added. "Is Victor Berríos connected to Carl Oxenwise?"

"Oxenwise is laundering the profits for Berríos," Scar explained.

"Did you toss Oxenwise's house?"

He shook his head.

"The Goon Squad did it?" I mused.

"They were there an hour before you showed up."

"Ha!" I exclaimed. "They followed us from the house."

"They followed you," he corrected snidely.

"You were still trailing me, so unless you missed them in front of you, then they had to be behind you."

He groaned.

"I still don't understand why they think you're involved," I pondered. "Are you?"

Scar shook his head. "I'm looking for the girl."

My eyebrows raised. "Of course. The pretty young girl on Bottlebrush Lane," I stated. "Victor Berríos is the boyfriend the neighbor saw?"

He nodded.

"What's the deal with the girl?" I asked.

"She's my daughter," Scar told me matter-of-factly.

8

"Your daughter?" I asked.

The man nodded, folding his hands on the table.

"I had no idea you were a daddy," I remarked.

"Cute," he blurted. "I've never met her."

"Never?" I stared at the enforcer.

Fatherhood never felt like it was attainable to me. Even if I met the person I thought would make an excellent mother, I wasn't so sure my qualifications were overly great. My role models were an abusive asshole and a drunk uncle. I'd steered away from those role models, but I did not design my life for kids.

However, I think if I'd had a child, I'd have been sure to be a part of their life.

As if he could read my mind, he explained, "In this world, a kid is a liability."

"That can't all be true," I commented.

"It's accurate enough," he confirmed. "I made enough enemies in my life to guarantee someone wants to hurt me. If anyone found out I had a daughter, they'd attempt to use her to force me to do something."

I lifted an eyebrow and laid my fork on the table. "Is that what's happening here?" I asked.

He shook his head. "Not entirely. No one knows Rosalina is my daughter."

"Rosalina?" I queried. "Pretty name."

He cocked his head and narrowed his eyes. "We aren't bonding over my family," he stated in a firm tone.

"Sorry," I offered with an apologetic gesture. "I just meant it sounded nice."

Scar scowled. "I didn't name her," he assured me, displaying the degree to which he was uninvolved.

"If you don't care so much, what are you doing?" I asked.

He shook his head. "I never said I didn't care."

I could see something in his eyes. A softness I'd never seen before. "I meant nothing by it," I apologized.

"I've stayed away for her safety," he assured me.

"Do you keep tabs on her?"

"Not really," he explained. "I provide for her. Beyond that, I have nothing to do with her or her mother."

"Does Moreno know?" I asked.

Scar shook his head. "No, it's best if no one knows." He locked eyes with me, stating, "Besides Rosalina's mother, you are now the only person who knows. I expect it to remain that way."

"Of course," I vowed. "I'm here to help only."

He stared at me.

Finally, he said, "Her mother called me two days ago. She has been told to never contact me. There's a bank account I put money in providing for Rosalina. She should never call me. When she did, it had to be because something was wrong."

I leaned in, paying attention. This was humanizing the killer.

He continued, "She told me Rosalina and Victor Berríos were together."

"How old is she?" I asked.

"Twenty."

"Too young to be mixed up with coke dealers," I remarked.

"Mmm," he groaned.

"Victor Berríos worked for Moralez?"

Scar nodded. "According to some people I've talked to. He was a runner. Picked up drops on his boat and brought them in. His father works for Moralez, too."

"A family business, huh?" I quipped.

Scar glared at me with humorless eyes. "His father is apparently loyal."

"You mean he'll give up his son to save face with Moralez?" I questioned.

"It's a dangerous world," Scar noted.

"You don't feel the same, though," I pointed out.

Scar frowned.

"I'm just saying," I explained, "you seem to help despite the trouble it might cause with Moreno."

His countenance twisted.

I shifted gears. "Berríos doesn't work for Moralez anymore?"

"From what I've heard," he confirmed. "However, I don't know why."

"You mean whether it was his choice or Moralez's?" I clarified.

"Or his father's," he added.

"So you found out Rosalina hooked up with Berríos, and that worried her mother?"

Scar finished the tequila in his glass and waved two fingers at the server, signaling his need for another one. Then, he explained, "Carla told me..."

"Carla is Rosalina's mother?" I asked.

"*Sí*. Yes."

"I understand that," I snipped.

The Cuban shrugged. "One should never underestimate the stupidity of *gringos*."

"Esteban, that might be offensive if it weren't true," I responded. "So, Carla told you what?"

"Rosalina gave her some money. She told her mother it was from a deal she and Berríos made. Word already spread that Moralez suspected Berríos of stealing his coke. It scared Carla."

"She thought you could do what?" I asked.

Scar folded his arms and gave me a stern stare that silently called me stupid again. As the server returned with another Milagro on the rocks, I shook my head.

"She expected you to remove Berríos," I commented.

"It was a thought," he agreed. "However, Moralez already connected Rosalina to Berríos. He's looking for either of them now."

"I'm guessing a man like Moralez doesn't care about the girl, either. Just his $5 million."

Scar agreed. "She's as guilty as Berríos. If he finds her, either she'll give up Berríos and the coke before he kills her or she doesn't. Both ways end with her dead."

"We could kill Moralez," I pointed out.

"That isn't an option."

"What happens if Moreno finds out?"

Scar stared at me without answering. He wasn't sure. There was no doubt in my mind that Esteban Velasquez would take a bullet for his boss, but he wasn't sure how the drug lord would react if his number two man's daughter was in danger.

Moreno counted on Scar to protect the drug lord's interests. A daughter would, as Scar pointed out, make him a weak link. Would a father always put the boss's business ahead of the well-being of family?

On the other hand, Moreno favored him. Maybe it was closer to a father-son relationship. In which case, Moreno might pull out all the stops to help Rosalina. Family is family, after all.

Scar's problem was doubt. He didn't have enough faith in Moreno to protect him. I didn't know him very well, but what I'd seen of Esteban Velasquez told me he was a man who could read people. His hesitation was probably justifiable.

The kicker was, while to me, five million dollars' worth of cocaine was a lot, to Moralez and Moreno, it might make up a week's worth of revenue. In corporate America, if a company lost a week's revenue, it would cost someone a job. If someone stole it, they might spend five to ten behind bars. They wouldn't get dragged out into the middle of the Gulf and dropped overboard with a slug in the back of their head.

"If you tell Julio, he might go to war for you," I told him.

"He might not," Scar retorted, confirming my suspicions of the man's distrust. "The toll might be too much."

"What if instead," I offered, "we kill Moralez, take the coke, and you disappear with Rosalina? Someplace out west."

"I'd do what?" he asked. "Pass myself off as Cherokee and work in a casino?"

"You'd have five million dollars. You could buy a trailer, park it in the desert, and never see a soul."

His expression told me it wasn't much of an option.

"We could find Rosalina and do the same with her, though. If we played it right, no one has to know she's your kid."

"What about Victor Berríos?" he asked.

"We hand him over to Moralez."

The enforcer studied me. "You'd do that?" he questioned.

I swallowed. The thought came to me so easily. As if this kid deserved to be killed. Not that stealing is justifiable, especially since all he's doing is redistributing the coke. He wanted his get-rich-quick scheme. Berríos probably wasn't much older than Rosalina.

"No, I wouldn't," I confirmed.

Scar smiled. It wasn't something I'd seen before. A genuine smile generated by mirth.

"This doesn't have to involve you," he finally told me after his grin passed.

"Eh," I murmured. "I need something to do."

He gave me an appreciative nod. There was an unusual air between us. I wondered if he found he trusted me more than he did Julio Moreno. Was this a crisis of faith for him? How long had he been with Moreno? Yet, here I was, a mere acquaintance, and I knew his deepest secret.

"What happened at the house?" I asked. "How did you find where they were living?"

"The guy I know suggested Oxenwise was laundering money for Berríos. It was more of a hunch," he explained. "When I went to the house, the two hitters were waiting for Berríos and Rosalina. I just arrived first."

"The couple never showed?" I asked.

He shrugged. "I wasn't the most inconspicuous in that neighborhood. The Karens don't appreciate my type hanging around unless we're cutting the grass."

"Don't forget the pools," I quipped.

"Yeah," he remarked. "Their husbands wouldn't appreciate a man with such distinct sexual prowess doing yardwork."

I eyed him with a smirk. "Did you just make a joke?"

With a deadpan expression, he blurted, "No."

I shook my head. The man was full of layers. "If we find Carl Oxenwise, we might find our little Bonnie and Clyde?" I asked.

His brow furrowed.

"Victor and Rosalina." Layers with very little trivial knowledge, apparently.

"Possibly."

"I guess it's safe to say he isn't at his house," I commented. "What else do you know about him?"

"He owns two laundromats," Scar told me. "That's where he launders the money."

"I wonder if the bastard did that on purpose," I quipped.

Scar still stared at me.

"Seriously," I gaped at him. "A laundromat that cleans money. It's a big pun. You could at least afford an eye roll."

He didn't respond.

"Have you checked them out?" I finally asked, breaking the awkward silence.

"Yeah. I've driven by, but I'd need to sit on either one of them to be sure he's not hiding in the back."

"Right, and it's difficult to watch two locations for any length of time," I acknowledged.

Scar grunted an agreement.

"But there's two of us now," I pointed out. "Why don't you take one, and I'll take the other?"

"Finish your food," he ordered. "I'll be back."

Without an explanation, he dropped a hundred-dollar bill on the table and left the restaurant. I finished eating. The fish was adequate–the kind of meal that disappoints because it's simply mediocre. I'd eaten a lot worse out of MREs, and the Corps taught me to eat when I could. It might be a while before the next meal.

Twenty minutes passed, and I ordered a slice of key lime *crème brûlée* while I waited on Scar. He sat back down with a plastic bag. He removed a prepaid phone from the bag, handing me the plastic cover to remove.

"You do know how to use it?" he questioned sardonically.

"Yeah," I retorted. "I get the general concept."

He gave me the address of Oxenwise's laundromat on the island. The plan was simple. We each sat outside a different store until we saw Oxenwise. People are creatures of habit and convenience. After the shooting on Bottlebrush Lane and the search of his house, Oxenwise would waver on the edge of fight or flight. Most people opt for the latter. It's easier. Especially if one has access to funds. He might have to hide out on three tons of quarters, but at least he had untraceable cash.

The two laundromats were on opposite ends of the island. Years ago, it would have surprised me that there would be two laundromats in such an affluent area, but since then, I've learned the value of convenient laundry. I can't fit a washing machine on *Carina*, so if I want clean clothes, it requires a bucket and elbow grease or a trip to a laundromat. Most decent marinas offer a laundry. But when I'm anchored out, I'll haul it ashore in my dinghy and trek to the nearest place.

With the bare bones of the plan in place, we took off in separate ways to find Oxenwise.

9

The South Seas Laundromat #3 was half a block from the Harbor Side Bar and Grill and amid rows of vacation rentals. I was almost at the northern tip of Captiva Island, close enough to see the Gulf of Mexico to the west, Pine Island Sound to the east, and, if I stretched my neck while standing on the hood of the Versa, the eight-hundred-foot stretch of Redfish Pass that separated Captiva Island from North Captiva Island. I hoped the cartographer who named the two islands did so because they were on one long stretch of land, not because they lacked the imagination to find an entirely different name.

Captiva was a bit of Florida I hadn't visited much. Just a little burg on a thin stretch of land protecting the mainland. Situated on the western coast, the barrier islands offered spectacular sunsets. Several of the local bars had countdown clocks to signal when it was time for the patrons to pull out their phones to snap pictures that would later grace Facebook and Instagram.

The islands offered a secluded piece of paradise. It was accessible by bridge, but it was enough out of the way to steer those rushing from Tampa to Naples from detouring to check out the scenery. However, it is never devoid of people. Snowbirds filtered down, filling the island around October and November, staying until spring warmed up their own states. Like so many other coastal areas of Florida, the island swarms with tourists between April and September. They are the blessing and the curse of all Floridians. These strangers swoop in demanding red-carpet treatment despite the fact they work for an insurance company in Springfield, Missouri or cut hair in Jasper, Alabama. When they cross the state line into Florida, they expect the royal treatment, ignoring common courtesy or local customs.

The bane is they pay the bills. They go to the cheesy beachside chain, where they drop a few hundred dollars off to a bartender or server. That money pays for the staff's apartment. The landlord takes that rent money and pays to get his oil changed. The mechanic uses his salary from the oil change to buy groceries. Even without taking into account the taxes the state and local governments steal, it is a cycle going on and on. It doesn't matter where the money ends up. Almost inevitably, it started in the hands of a tourist.

Nothing drives vitriol for a group of people more than being beholden to them for something. Humans want to consider ourselves self-sufficient. It's a rarity to find a person who is. Almost universally, we require something from someone else. It's been that way since the first few humans roomed together in a cave in France.

It took over two hours of sitting for my brain to meander around like that. There was only so much interest the dirty windows of a laundromat could sustain.

Luckily, I couldn't ask for a better day to sit in the parking lot of the laundromat. The weather was perfect–sunny with a gentle breeze. My windows were down, allowing the wind across the water to carry the smell of salt and sea. The radio played a classic rock station out of Tampa, and the Doors were reiterating my own thoughts–people are strange. If I could stomach the third commercial in the last hour advertising testosterone treatments, I might hear Mick tell me the things I want aren't always available or Steven relating the story of Janie killing her rapist father.

After we scoped out both locations, we found a hotel off the island. Scar wanted to sit on the laundromats all night, but I didn't think we'd have any luck overnight. Besides, we needed some rest.

Scar found a picture of Carl Oxenwise on the man's Facebook page. Based on the picture, he was not a modest man. He was in his early forties and pushing 275 pounds. Very little of it was muscle. He had missed a few of his Zumba classes over the last few years. Despite the obvious softness of the man, if you looked at the photos he voluntarily shared on his social media, the man wasn't scared of a Speedo.

To avoid thoughts of Oxenwise's defiance of nylon's stretching capacity, I considered Scar's conundrum. It made sense why he stayed away from Rosalina. Somehow, while he never said it, there was some sense of fatherly duty there. Where did that come from? My father was around throughout my childhood, and he never showed an inkling of duty, love, or desire to be there. How did a thug like Esteban Velasquez, who had killed countless people for crossing paths with him, have the capacity to protect a daughter that didn't know he existed?

The question hung there. Unanswerable. Which added to the reasons I doubted my own abilities as a father. If I had a kid, what would that do to me? I couldn't shake the image of my father, and it wasn't a reflection I ever wanted to see. The best defense to me seemed to be avoidance.

A door on the back wall of the laundromat opened. I had seen no one come and go from there until now. A rotund man in a Guy Harvey print shirt came out. He scanned the machines where three women and a kid were. Two of the women were watching the washers while the other was ironing a pile of clothes she'd just removed from the dryer.

Despite not sporting a too tiny thong, Carl Oxenwise was easily recognizable. He was carrying a large canvas bag like one sees armored truck guards use. Oxenwise moved around the store, removing the coins from each machine. His head swiveled nervously as he continuously checked the room to make sure the customers hadn't shifted positions.

It was conceivable he was always nervous when pulling the money from the machines. It would be a lot of quarters, which could add up. If someone knew the times he did the withdrawals, it would make for an easy cash grab.

Somehow, this seemed like abnormal anxiety.

I reached for the phone to text Scar. We were checking in hourly no matter what, but should one of us spot

Oxenwise, we'd alert the other. He was almost twelve miles away, stationed near Sanibel, on the other end of the island chain. I'd sit on Oxenwise until he showed up, unless something happened.

As I sent the text though, something happened.

The Goon Squad showed up. Just Goon One and Two. The one whose wrist I broke wasn't with them.

The two giants strolled up the sidewalk and entered the store. I glanced around, trying to figure out where they'd come from. The parking lot was minuscule, and yet for the second time, they showed up without my seeing them. I couldn't even spot a car big enough for the Goon Brothers.

It took less than ten seconds for the four customers to come running from the store as the goons began throwing things around. A shouting Goon One bounced about like an animation, and Oxenwise cowered in the corner, fumbling with the canvas bag.

"Shit," I hissed, reaching into the backseat to retrieve my M45 from the bag.

I held the gun low as I rushed from the rental car to the door. As soon as I entered, the electronic bell dinged, alerting everyone to my entrance.

All three men seemed to turn and stare at me. My hand came up, pointing the M45 at Goon One.

"Gentlemen," I blurted out. "I think we need to stop running into each other."

Goon One locked eyes with me, but Goon Two swept his head around, no doubt looking for Scar. That was Two's mistake. All hell broke loose.

Oxenwise pulled a .22 automatic from the canvas bag and fired three shots at Goon Two. The little launderer was nervous, but all three shots hit Two in the chest.

As my eyes shifted for a split second to the falling man, Goon One came up with another 9 mm, having replaced the one Scar and I took off him, and shot Oxenwise. As he turned toward me, I dove behind a row of washing machines.

The gunshots echoed through the store, but I still felt the impact of bullets striking the machines. I crawled along the back side of the machines as Goon One continued to fire. The shots varied, and I guessed he checked on Goon Two between spurts of gunfire.

I wanted to get to Oxenwise, and as long as Goon One was firing at me, he was not shooting at the wounded man. I fired two shots between a gap in the machines. The click of a new magazine slamming into the Glock signaled a fresh round of gunfire. I fired over the top of the machine, shooting three rounds before scampering a few feet away. The metal washing machines were a perfect barrier. It wasn't likely a 9 mm round could punch through the entire thing, and if I kept moving, he might spend his ammunition out of sheer rage.

"Take your brother and go," I shouted before shifting positions.

"Not before I gut that little fucker," he howled.

Great, he was moving for Oxenwise. I popped up, firing. The big man dropped behind another row.

"That will not happen," I told him as I moved toward Oxenwise.

I was still behind the washers, but I had a clear line of sight to the chunky man. He was bleeding heavily from his right arm, and I realized the bullet must have torn open his brachial artery. He needed attention soon, or he'd bleed out.

There wasn't much chance of Scar popping in as backup. With the traffic on the island, it would take him half an hour to make the drive from Sanibel to here.

Of course, the goon didn't need to know that.

"You better go now," I warned. "I have reinforcements."

"Where is Velasquez?" he hissed.

"He just walked up the street for a burger about fifteen minutes ago. I don't think you want to be here when he gets back."

As if out of pure hatred, the beast stood and fired repeatedly toward me. I lost count around thirteen shots, but he must have unloaded the clip into the washer I was hiding behind.

The doorbell dinged as he retreated from the laundromat. After a few seconds of silence, I peered over to see the laundromat empty.

I raced over to Oxenwise, who was marinating in a pool of his own blood. The brachial artery pumps a great deal of blood through the arms, and if it's cut, it doesn't take long for the heart to push enough blood out to exsanguinate a body. My eyes scanned the area. The woman who fled the building left her basket of clothes. On the heap was a black tank top. I ripped it down the middle and wrapped it around Oxenwise's upper arm. The ends of the cloth wound around the barrel of his .22, which I turned. The tourniquet tightened as I twisted the gun. It slowed the bleeding, but he'd lost a lot of blood. The binding would not stop enough.

"Dammit," I growled.

I sprinted to the other side of the room where the woman had been ironing. The iron was still hot. With a quick tug, I jerked the cord from the outlet and bolted across the room.

The plate was still hot, and it seared Oxenwise's skin when I pressed it against it. He was lucky he was unconscious, as the skin melted to conform to the point of the iron. I hoped it cauterized the artery enough to sustain him until the paramedics arrived.

There wasn't much point in leaving. The witnesses would have seen my Versa in the lot, and Oxenwise had three cameras covering the laundromat. It would be tough to hide my presence.

While I assumed at least one of the fleeing customers called the police, I walked over to the store's phone on the wall and dialed 911. Oxenwise was as stable as I could make him, so I waited for the police or ambulance to show up first.

10

In a perfect world, the cops would show up, see how I stabilized Oxenwise, and let me go.

We don't live under such idyllic circumstances. Instead, two uniformed police officers arrived on scene with their guns drawn. Since I have zero desire to be mistaken as an armed combatant, I sat in a chair next to the dying Carl Oxenwise with my M45 resting on top of a dryer. I laced together both of my hands on the back of my head.

The officers called an ambulance, but not until an officer handcuffed and placed me in the back of a squad car. It was a precaution until the police established a semblance of order to the crime scene.

I watched the paramedics wheel Oxenwise from the laundromat. Had he lost too much blood? I hoped I'd staunched it off long enough to save him. The siren blared on the ambulance as it sped away from the building.

Then it was just a matter of waiting.

Handcuffed with my wrists at my back wasn't the ideal position for sitting around in the back of a dingy police car. The Captiva police didn't clean the back of the squad car much. Something crusty was sticking to the floor, and from the appearance, I guessed it was dried vomit from sometime long ago.

More officers arrived on scene. Shootouts would not be common in a little community like Captiva Island. That meant every on-duty officer wanted to pass through it. They needed stories for the future when someone offered to buy the man in blue a beer.

Before the first half hour passed, the officer who put me in the back of the car returned.

"Mr. Gordon?" he asked. I wasn't sure if he was reminding himself of my name or verifying the subject in his car was still the same one he'd locked up. Maybe it was a sneaky interrogation technique to trick me into revealing I'd given them a pseudonym.

Whatever it was, I nodded. Let him figure that out.

"Want to tell me what happened here?" he asked when he slid into the front seat. He turned to look at me through an opening in the plastic separating the front from the back seat.

He was a career officer, happy to spend a couple of decades policing a peaceful community on the ocean side. Even though his average day comprised DUIs with the occasional disturbing the peace complaint, the cop looked like he was ready to storm a compound. Between the Kevlar and the daily weight training, he appeared thicker above the waist. His hair was graying, but only around the temples. The officer's blue eyes were hypnotizing–somewhere between a sky blue and aqua.

"Could you crack a window or turn the air up?" I asked. "It's beyond stuffy in here."

He reached forward and adjusted a setting on the controls. A breeze blew from under the seat, cooling the still air I'd been breathing.

"Better?" he asked.

"Thanks," I acknowledged.

"So, what happened?"

"I was sitting in my car over there when these two men charged into the laundromat. The customers inside ran out, and I thought it was some kind of robbery. I thought the poor man inside was in trouble, and I went in to help."

"With your firearm?" he questioned.

"Yes," I confirmed. "My permit is in my wallet."

"It's a nice .45," he commented. "I don't see a lot of M45s out there. You a Marine?"

"Used to be," I told him.

"Doesn't that just mean, yes?"

I shrugged. "You know how people are," I pointed out, expecting him to understand what I meant.

"I got out in '04," he remarked. "Should have stayed for my twenty."

"Why didn't you?" I asked. Now we were becoming friends. Of course, that could be a trick. They teach every officer to connect with the subject. Make nice and see what they say. I could play that game if he wanted.

"Ex-wife got pregnant," he stated. "She thought I should be home more. Three years later, she left me for some guy in the Navy."

"Fucking squids," I joked. "Can't even get their own women."

"Damn straight," he smiled.

"There were several customers that saw me go in after the fact," I told him, changing gears.

"We're looking into that," he informed me. "Says you live in West Palm. What are you doing here?"

This was the one question there wasn't a suitable answer to. If I stuck to the details of what happened, I knew the truth would stand. Both victims shot each other, and while I discharged my weapon, the cops would find none of my bullets in anybody. Unless Goon One stumbled into an emergency room somewhere, and I knew I never hit him.

But I don't think I can tell the officer I found myself caught between the Moreno and Moralez cartels. He'd given me half an hour to consider my story.

"I'm off a few days," I lied. "I was waiting to meet a friend."

"What is your friend's name?" he asked.

My face contorted on purpose. "Uh, she's... uh... married," I stammered. "You can call Jay Delp over at the Palm County Sheriff. He can vouch for me."

"It'd help you more if you gave me your friend's name," he offered sternly.

I sighed, saying, "I'd rather not. Unless I'm forced to."

His eyes narrowed. "Why were you waiting in the laundromat's parking lot?" he asked.

I shrugged sheepishly, explaining, "Waiting for her to give me the all-clear."

He shook his head, and I added with a smile, "If it helps, her husband is a politician."

"How does that help?" he asked.

"He's busy screwing everyone else?" I quipped.

The cop shook his head with half a smile. "The detective will want to talk to you," he told me. "I'll get back to you."

When he left, I sat back on my hands, which were falling asleep. More cars arrived while I had talked to the officer. The entire police department was making its appearance. This was prime drama, and it would be a measure to mark the passage of time. Time would turn it into a massacre, even if Oxenwise survived. With any luck, I'd become a hero of urban legend.

While I sat in the back of the squad car, I wondered if the cop regretted leaving the Corps to have a kid. Some days I missed it, but not in the sense I want to do it again. My time passed there. Life offers lots of changes, and when the realization that a certain period of your life has died, it becomes freeing. I didn't regret leaving the Corps, even though I loved that time in my life.

If I'd just traded the Corps for another institution, I think I'd hate it. That would just be substituting one thing for another, and that results in misery and resentment.

I twisted around and rested my head on the window. Given the detail not addressed in cleaning this car, I should have been leery of touching too many surfaces.

Where was Scar? I texted him before the cops arrived, and then I smashed the phone and kicked the pieces under several washing machines. Oxenwise had cameras installed in the laundromat, but I took advantage of a blind spot to destroy the phone. Hopefully the police wouldn't find it, but even if they did, I could deny it.

By now, he should have made it up here from Sanibel. I peered out the window, searching for his face in the crowd milling at the edge of the parking lot. Everyone's vacation skidded to a stop so they could marvel at a live action depiction of Law and Order.

A guy in his late thirties walked toward the squad car. His hair thinned on top, and he sported aviator sunglasses and a light blue polo—standard Florida uniform for plain-clothes cops.

He opened the rear door. "Chase Gordon?" he asked.

"Yeah," I responded again, still wondering what the question really meant.

"Why don't you step out?" he offered, as if he was bending a rule to make me more comfortable.

Had his intent been to offer me some solace, he might have unlocked the cuffs, so I didn't look like a wounded sea lion trying to pull myself out of the back seat with both hands behind my back.

"Officer James gave me your statement," he told me. James, I assumed, was the former Marine whose wife ran off. I didn't clarify with the man, nodding instead.

"I'm Detective Wrencher," he introduced.

"Think I could get out of these?" I asked, turning to motion with my wrists.

As if the idea never dawned on him, he bobbed his head. "Absolutely," he responded, reaching into his pocket for a key ring. "I talked with Detective Delp over at Palm County."

"I hope he gave me a glowing review," I commented.

"'Glowing' might not be the word I would use," Wrencher replied. "He asked whose wife you were sleeping with."

"In fairness, this is the only wife I'm sleeping with," I explained.

"One witness described how you ran in after the two men came in," Wrencher detailed. "She ducked behind her car and watched. Sounds like you were in the right place at the right time."

"That depends on your point of view," I countered. "I had better plans for this afternoon."

He scowled a bit, and I wondered if I was edging around a touchy subject with him. Unfortunately, I'd already committed to the lie.

"Well, for the owner, it seems you came in at the right time."

"Is he going to be okay?" I asked.

Wrencher shook his head. "I'm not sure," he answered. "We haven't heard his condition. Why did you run inside when everyone else was coming out?"

"Instinct," I told him. "I saw the trouble, and someone had to help."

"You could have called us," he suggested.

"I did," I responded. "It took nine minutes for the first officers to arrive. That's a long time. Since it took about two minutes from the time the two men entered the laundromat until the one ran out, I don't think you guys could have made it in time."

"I pulled your record," he told me. "You had quite a career in the Marines. Now, you're just a bartender."

"I wasn't looking for a career anywhere," I replied.

"Still," he continued, "why the big change?"

"I wanted to do and go where I wanted."

He nodded as if he understood the sentiment. I didn't think he did, but then again, I've long stopped trying to explain my lifestyle to anyone.

"How long are you in the area?" he asked.

"Just for the day."

"Do you have a contact number?" he asked, pulling a pad out.

"Not really," I told him. "You can call the Manta Club at the Tilly Inn in West Palm Beach. Most of my calls go there."

"You don't have a cell phone?" he questioned with a furrowed brow.

I shook my head. "No, I don't like the idea of being tethered. Never had one in the Corps, and it made little sense to get one when I got out."

His face had the same confused look most people shared when they learned I didn't have a phone. "What if someone needs to reach you?" he asked.

"They can leave a message for me at the Manta Club."

"In an emergency?" he continued. "Like what if your mom wants to call?"

"That's just another reason not to have one," I retorted.

"I'm going to ask you not to leave the state then," he informed me.

"But I'm not under arrest?" I asked.

"Not right now. There will be an investigation, but the witness corroborates your story."

I nodded along with a congenial expression. If he didn't arrest me, he couldn't demand I stay in the state. However, I didn't have to make a fuss about it. Let the man imply a certain authority.

"We have to keep your gun, though," he told me. "Until we complete the investigation."

"Absolutely," I told him, knowing the investigation could take months, even years. I'd have to write that gun off for the time being.

"If you'll call me tomorrow or the next day, I'd like to touch base in case any more questions arise."

I agreed before he changed his mind.

11

Prudence suggested getting off Captiva Island before Detective Wrencher thought he had more questions for me. The only way off was south through Sanibel to the causeway, connecting to the mainland. When I reached Sanibel, I pulled over at a 7-Eleven that still had a pay phone.

It took a dollar's worth of quarters, but I called Jay.

"What kind of trouble are you in?" he asked before I could greet him.

"Not a lot, now," I remarked. "Thanks to you."

"A double shooting isn't a lot of trouble?"

"Technically, I didn't shoot anyone," I pointed out.

"Your Detective Wrencher wasn't so sure of that," he commented. "I assured him that if you shot anyone, it was justified. I told him to look up your record, too."

"What would that prove to him?" I asked.

"If you were the one that started shooting, then the other guy wouldn't have gotten away."

I scoffed at him.

"Seriously, Flash, is this about Velasquez?"

"It's very complicated," I explained.

"Well, I left out the drug dealers when I talked to Wrencher," he informed me. "It better not come back and bite me in the ass."

I sighed. "About that," I began. "Can you tell me if Victor Berríos has any kind of record?"

"Victor Berríos?" Jay asked. "Who is he?"

"Do you want to know everything, Jay?"

He inhaled a deep breath. Ignoring my question, he repeated, "Victor Berríos?"

I spelled the name, and I could hear him typing.

"Victor Berríos. Twenty years old. Tampa PD arrested him two years ago on possession with intent. His lawyer pleaded him down to a year of probation. There isn't an employer listed, but I'd need to go through the probation records to find that information. It's been a year now, so that might not be accurate, anyway. His address is in Tampa."

He gave me the address. Obviously, he had moved from the address since he was living in Oxenwise's house. However, if he was eighteen when the possession charge hit him, it wasn't unreasonable to assume the address in question belonged to his parents. Where else might one go if they were running scared?

"Be careful, Chase," Jay warned. "I don't need to come identify your body."

"Don't worry, Jay," I assured him. "I think, if it's Moralez that does me in, there won't be much to identify."

"Encouraging," he remarked as he hung up.

I dumped another four quarters into the pay phone.

"Took you long enough," Scar stated when he answered.

"I had to ditch the phone," I told him.

"Good," he acknowledged. "Oxenwise dead?"

"The police said he was heading to the hospital in critical condition."

"Damn, Gordon," he hissed. "Did you find out anything?"

"I have an address for Berríos," I told him.

"From Oxenwise?" he asked.

"No, I called Jay."

Scar groaned. "Could've saved us some time," he pointed out.

I ignored him. "I'm in Sanibel. We can meet somewhere."

"Get over to Fort Myers," he ordered. "I'll pick you up."

I was only a twenty-minute ride across the causeway, and when I reached our rendezvous, I was early. A taco shop in the strip mall offered ninety-nine cent chicken tacos. After buying four, I sat on the hood of my Versa, waiting and eating. Half an hour later, Scar's Lexus pulled into the shopping center's parking lot.

"You have the address?" he asked as he rolled his window down.

"Not even a 'hello' or 'glad you're not in jail.'"

He scowled at me.

"My mother always said if you make those faces, they'll stick that way," I commented. "Of course, I wouldn't listen to her. She was a bitch."

"Get in the damn car, Gordon," he growled.

I told him where to go as I shut the door. He pulled a plastic bag from between the seats and handed it to me.

"Another phone," I blurted out, mimicking excitement.

"Try not to lose it," he ordered.

My fingers pried the plastic package apart.

"I talked with a guy after you called. Oxenwise is in surgery."

I turned to face the man. "You have a guy in the hospital?"

He scoffed. "We do business up here. It would be foolish not to cultivate sources."

I only nodded. "Is he going to make it?"

Scar shrugged. "Sounds like he might lose his arm."

A shiver passed over me. I wondered if my haste to cauterize the vessel resulted in more damage. Not that it mattered. If I hadn't acted, Oxenwise would not have survived long enough to get off the grungy tile floor.

"Moralez's man is dead," he informed me.

"I know," I assured him. "Oxenwise pulled a little .22. Hit him square."

"The cameras in the store were all fake," he explained.

"That makes some sense," I remarked. "It's an illusion of security, but it records nothing he's doing."

"Seems foolish," Scar noted.

"If he was paranoid, he might worry that the IRS or FBI might get a warrant to review his footage. It might be enough to catch him in the act."

"What act?" Scar pondered. "He launders money."

"I'm no expert," I pointed out. "But a laundromat might make a perfect place. He simply brings the money in and calls it profits. It's an all-cash business. Who could say how much he makes? If it gets to be too much money, he opens another location."

"So why not have cameras?"

"They might dispute how much business he actually has."

Scar scoffed again. Obviously, he didn't buy into my theory. Of course, between the two of us, he was more adept at criminal behavior.

"The point is he doesn't have cameras, so the cops can't see what happened," I surmised.

"Should make it look like a robbery, not a targeted assault," Scar said.

He drove north toward Tampa. The ride was mostly silent. The drug enforcer had little to say, and he shut down any attempt I made at starting a conversation with a one-word answer or nothing at all.

I wondered how his mind worked. Did Esteban Velasquez have any close friends? Right now, it seemed even his boss turned his back on him. Although, I wasn't certain that was the case. This wasn't a betrayal of Moreno, and if the drug lord knew the circumstances, he might come to his lieutenant's aid.

Of course, I didn't know enough about that life. I might attribute Moreno with regular human traits the man didn't have.

Whatever the answer was, didn't matter. For the moment, I was along for the ride.

My attention turned out the window as we crossed the Tampa city limits.

12

The address for Victor Berríos was a Spanish single-story home on a middle-class street. While the house appeared to be maintained with care, it was modest compared to the ones owned by Oxenwise. Neatly trimmed roses adorned the front flower beds demarcated with white agatized coral found all over this part of Florida.

"If this is his parents' house, you'll need to go do the talking," Scar informed me as he parked the Lexus down the street.

I looked over at him with a curious glance.

He waved his hand over his face, saying, "Some people will recognize me as *Señor* Moreno's second."

"They might not talk to you?" I questioned. "I figured that intimidated most people."

"They might prefer to shoot me. Or worse, cut their losses," he advised.

I assumed he meant Rosalina. Scar worried more about Rosalina's safety than mine.

He added, "You, though. You are just a dumb *gringo.*"

"Thanks," I remarked. "That doesn't mean they won't try to kill me."

He handed me a Glock 9 mm.

"Think there will be trouble?" I asked, checking the action on the 9 mm.

"Berríos's father worked for Moralez," he pointed out. "Best to assume the worst."

I nodded. As I got out of the Lexus, I slipped the Glock into my waistband.

"Try to be careful," Scar suggested. "I'm not coming in after you."

"That's not what I expect a partner to say," I told him. "Haven't you watched a single buddy cop movie?"

He groaned, saying, "I don't like cops, even in movies."

"Are you saying you never watched Lethal Weapon or Bad Boys?"

He shook his head. "No, but I pulled for Gary Busey."

"Dude," I exclaimed. "No one roots for Gary Busey."

His eyes narrowed on me, and I laughed. His delivery was dry and on-point.

I followed the sidewalk next to the rose-bushes and knocked on the carved wooden door. After a few seconds, the door opened, and an attractive Latino woman in her early forties stared back at me with deep mahogany-colored eyes. She was nearly a foot shorter than me, with a small frame.

"Hello," I greeted with a smile. "I'm looking for Victor."

"Victor?" she asked, raising her eyebrows.

"Yes, Victor Berríos. I'm with the probation office," I explained, hoping to deliver enough fear for her to cooperate.

"Probation?" she questioned with a worried brow that told me my ruse was working. "Is everything okay?"

"Oh, yes," I assured her. "There is some paperwork we need from Victor to close out his case and issue a refund."

I have never faced probation, but I guessed the legal work involved cost a few bucks. I hoped that a promise of a refund would spur this woman to direct me to her son. Combine that with the authority behind a probation officer, and a mother might be more willing to cooperate.

"Why is there a refund?" she asked.

I shrugged. "Who knows?" I questioned, appealing to the great unknown. "It's likely Victor overpaid at some point. You know how the government is. We take our time doing anything."

"How much is it?" she asked with eager eyes.

I shook my head. "I'm sorry. Since Victor is an adult, I can only talk to him about it. It's not a paltry sum, though. Is he available?"

"He is not here," she told me apologetically.

"Can you call him?" I asked. "It would be nice to get this cleared up today. He'd probably like a few thousand dollars, too."

I made a face as if I accidentally let the amount slip out.

"Would you like to come in?" she offered. "I can call him."

"That would be lovely," I assured her. "What was your name?"

"Jovina," she told me. "Victor is my son."

"You are too young to have a son his age," I told her.

Her face reddened a tint as she ushered me inside.

The inside of her house was clean, as if she was expecting company. The decor appeared out of place for the modest home. Most of the furniture was new–less than a year old. An entertainment system filled the front room with an one-hundred-inch television and sound system that cost ten thousand dollars retail. Most of the curios were a hodgepodge collection gathered from high-end shops. Crystal figurines bearing emblems saying Swarovski lined the mantel.

"Would you like some coffee?" she offered. Her accent was still noticeable, however it was obvious she practiced her diction.

"Please," I responded with a gracious smile.

"I'll call Victor," she promised. "He's really trying to be a better person."

"Good," I told her. "It's nice to see the system work for someone. What's he doing now?"

She walked into the other room as she answered, "He's working as a divemaster. He's hoping to get his own boat soon."

"That's ambitious," I commented as I moved around the room.

Pictures lined several shelves. Most were in cheap Kmart frames, which was a stark transition to the expensive pieces filtered around the room.

A younger version of Jovina stood with another Latino man and a teenaged boy–Victor, I presumed. The man must have been his father, the hitter for Moralez. Another photo showed an older Victor wearing a wet suit peeled down to his waist. He held a snapper up in a victorious pose for the camera. He was on the deck of a boat docked in what appeared to be Tampa Bay. The outline of the Marriott hotel loomed behind his smiling face.

"Where is he diving now?" I asked.

"Oh," she responded from the kitchen. "He's doing charters. I think down south a bit. He has a partnership with some guy."

There were other pictures of Victor ranging from infant to high school. Several centered on the beach or near water. He must have grown up with a love of the water. Maybe selling off Moralez's coke was his business plan. Get enough money to buy his own boat.

I could appreciate the concept. While Jovina seemed lovely enough, looks are often deceptive. I've been on the opposite end of that, and if stealing a brick of cocaine would get me out, the prospect would tempt me, too. Luckily, the Corps offered me an escape.

Here I was, putting my own thoughts on someone. I liked the smiling Victor, with his fresh catch. If he was likable, I could justify helping him. In fact, it would almost seem like a necessity.

"Do you like cream and sugar?" she asked.

"Black is fine," I answered.

"I messaged Victor," she told me as she returned with two cups. "He'll be here in just a few minutes."

"Great," I told her, taking the cup she offered. "You have a lovely home. How long have you lived here?"

"Since 1999," she answered. "Victor's father bought us the house when we got married."

"What does he do?" I asked congenially, attempting to play the part of a curious probation officer.

"He works for a seafood company," she answered.

Did she know the truth? Or had the lie been told so many times it was rote?

A door opened in the kitchen, and three men walked into the den. Goon One stood on the side of the man from the Berríos family picture with another man I had never seen.

The coffee cup fell from my hand as I rose, reaching for the Glock.

Goon One hissed, "Don't." He held a similar Glock pointing in my direction.

"You're the *gringo* killing everyone?" the senior Berríos commented.

I lifted my hands. "In fairness, I didn't kill the last guy. And I've yet to kill him," I remarked, pointing at Goon One.

The beast's fist flew forward and hit me. I fell onto a shelf, sending several crystal statues to the ground.

"*¡Maldita sea!*" Jovina shouted. "You're destroying my stuff."

"*Lo siento, mi amore,*" senior Berríos apologized. "Pick him up."

Goon One grabbed my arm and hoisted me up like a rag doll. He plucked the Glock from my waist and dropped me on my feet.

Senior Berríos stepped forward. "Where is my son?" he questioned, spewing spittle toward me.

"If I knew where he was, I wouldn't be here looking for him," I remarked.

"Where is the cocaine?" Senior Berríos asked. "Or Velasquez?"

"Listen," I offered. "I don't even like Velasquez. And you guys are the ones that dragged me into this shit."

"You work for Moreno," Berríos responded.

"I'm a bartender," I retorted.

"That's a lie," Goon One declared. "You were at Moreno's."

"That doesn't mean I work for him," I explained.

"Why are you looking for Victor?" Jovina demanded.

"Since people started trying to kidnap me and kill me, I've just wanted to figure out what the hell is going on. Victor seems to be at the center."

"*No me importa*," the elder Berríos replied. "If you aren't useful, we'll get rid of you."

He motioned for them to follow him. Goon One pushed me toward the door.

I glanced over my shoulder at Jovina. "You realize they'll end up killing Victor," I commented.

Goon One slammed his fist down on me, pushing me to the floor. He jerked me back to my feet. "Move," he hissed in my ear.

"I'm trying not to have any hard feelings here," I told him. "But I'm thinking you don't like me much."

The giant grunted and shoved me out the back door. The Berríos patriarch led us down an alley behind the house, eliminating much chance of Scar seeing us.

"*Señor* Berríos?" I questioned. "I didn't get your first name."

"*¡Veta a la mierda!*" he snapped. Based on the tone, I assumed it wasn't something polite.

A large black Lincoln sat on the street. I took two glances up both sides of the street, looking for Scar's Lexus. No sign of it. Of course, the man was elusive. He could have eyes on me now. However, was he ruthless enough simply to use me as bait? Or could I count on him to save me?

Goon One, who now seemed to have a superfluous moniker since his twin's demise, pushed me through the door. He squeezed in next to me, taking up the rest of the back seat. A man his size is impossible to fight in a confined space. I could hit him all day, and unless the blow was lethal, he'd likely only get angrier. I needed leverage if I wanted a chance against him, and the back seat of a Lincoln was like wrestling in a sardine can.

Berríos got into the front passenger seat while the third man drove.

"Did Victor steer away from the family values because you didn't give him enough attention?" I queried.

The senior Berríos twisted in his seat with a sneer. "The boy thought he deserved everything," he growled.

"Damned millennials," I snapped. "Am I right?"

"Shut up," Goon ordered.

"Is his mama okay with you murdering her boy?" I asked.

"What I do with my son is no concern of yours," he replied.

"Oh, I can relate. Don't worry," I told him.

The man turned his head again, curiously.

"My father was a raging asshole, too," I commented. "Your kid deserves some credit. I don't think I would have had the balls to stand up to him like he did. Moralez isn't happy with you either, right?"

"Shut up," Goon shouted.

I ignored the man. "Of course, your son, your problem. Of course, if you don't find the coke or Victor, Moralez might blame you."

Berríos glanced at Goon with menacing eyes. I saw the elbow jab coming, but couldn't block it in the confined space. The blow knocked my head back and everything swirled into blackness.

13

Two hands dragged me from the back of the Lincoln. The Florida sun forced me to squint, blocking its rays.

"Get up," Goon demanded, pulling me up to my feet.

I was still coming back around. Goon's strike left me unconscious for several minutes, and I needed to get my bearings.

Besides the aching head, the first thing I noticed was the aroma of fish. Dead fish. The odor was followed by a familiar clanging of metal. They dragged me to a marina.

Even with a jumbled brain, I had a good idea of what the three men planned for me. Why bother hiding a body on land when just to the west of us millions of square miles of ocean offered the perfect hiding place? The water doesn't need to be that deep, twenty feet or more. Dump the corpse with some weight and leave it for the scavengers at the bottom of the sea. It would make a needle in a haystack seem like a piece of cake.

"Move it," Goon pushed me forward.

He stayed behind me. As soon as he shoved me, he stepped back out of reach. If I was going to attack him, I needed to get him while he stepped closer. Right now, my equilibrium was out of whack, which meant I didn't trust any opening Goon might give me yet.

Where are you, Scar? I hoped he noticed the black Lincoln. But Berríos parked it on the next street over. He didn't want to be seen coming and going from his own house. Was he being watched by someone besides Scar? I could have been right. Moralez might blame him for Victor's actions. An affront like stealing over five million dollars' worth of cocaine had to be accounted for. Otherwise, everyone might think it's okay to take from Moralez. It's a poor policy for a drug lord to allow those impressions to exist. Consequences will occur.

Victor's father might not have the sort of fatherly trait one hears about–a paternal love strong enough to sacrifice one's self for their child. I've never seen it firsthand. My dad would trade my health and well-being for a pack of menthols.

As my pupils adjusted for the sun, I marched toward the small marina as Goon prodded me forward. Several fishing boats occupied the covered slips. Unfortunately, the docks were empty.

Blood stained the wooden table where fishermen skinned and filleted the fresh catch of the day. A pump under the table pulled water from the bay up to wash off the remaining guts. The air was pungent, almost over-bearing, with the aroma of rotting fish.

Berríos and the other man led us to the second slip where an older model center-console nineteen-foot Boston Whaler floated. The logo on the side was barely visible after years of rubbing against fenders and docks. Brown scuffs and scratches marked the years of weather beating the boat against the wooden pylons. Two 250-horsepower outboard engines hung on the transom, offering far more speed than a tarpon or tuna required.

Berríos followed the other man as they climbed aboard.

"A boat ride?" I asked. "I'm not sure that's in my best interest."

"Get in," Goon countered.

"We can shoot you here," Berríos offered, "or there."

I glanced around the dock. There were only six slips, and no one was around to witness my murder. Even the parking lot was empty. The only vehicle was the black Lincoln we arrived in.

I shrugged. "At least I get a boat ride," I commented as I stepped into the bow of the boat. "Do I get to ride up front at least?"

"Whatever," Berríos responded as Goon rocked the vessel when he climbed aboard.

The barrel of Goon's Glock remained level with me. The third man must drive everywhere. He started the engines on the Boston Whaler as Berríos untied the dock lines. The big outboards rumbled to life, shaking the entire boat. The driver deftly backed the boat out of the slip. As the bow was almost clear of the fingers, he pushed the starboard engine's throttle forward, spinning the boat ninety degrees starboard and aiming the bow toward the mouth of the inlet.

As the fishing boat pushed out of the pass, the waves increased. A southerly wind created a heavy chop. The twin outboards drove the hull through the waves, but not without the constant rising and falling over the crests.

My knees bent and straightened on instinct as I anticipated the waves. Life aboard gave me sea legs. So much so, when I was back on land, I often felt phantom waves which I figured was my body expecting something that wasn't there. Of course, even being used to waves didn't leave me immune to the physics of being tossed around. I was just a little more used to it.

Goon, however, wasn't. His face betrayed the fact he wasn't a fan of the motion. He might not have liked the water at all, but that was hard to judge. He could have been developing a case of sea sickness. I only experienced it once during my first month of cruising. It might have been the worst feeling I'd endured.

The driver continued out of the bay, steering clear of other boats. It was probably a strategic path to avoid anyone getting close enough to see me held at gunpoint. The meandering course wasn't helping Goon's color.

They were going to take me out of the bay, otherwise my body might wash up sooner. If I were the one dumping a body, I'd go at least five to ten miles out. Rescuers have enough trouble finding conscious victims out from shore that far. A body would be nearly impossible to find. Of course, long odds paid out occasionally.

I didn't want to get five to ten miles out. The only way to get out of this was to find a gap and attack.

The obstacle was the Goon. I needed to disarm and subdue him before Berríos reacted. Taking the Glock from him wouldn't be hard, but the brute could pack a punch, meaning I still had to deal with him. If I figured a second or two to take the gun, he had a second or two to land a blow that might knock me off the boat.

Now that we were moving away from shore, the swells lofted the fishing boat over each crest. The air felt like a storm might come on that southerly breeze. It could be hours, maybe even a day out, but it was there. The water churned as the wind pushed over the sea.

Both engines whined each time the props came out of the water as the boat crested each wave. The driver wasn't compensating for each rise and fall. They were in a rush to ditch me either before a random Fish and Wildlife officer pulled them over for a routine check or I caused problems.

Goon wasn't handling the sea conditions the same way the other two did. Goon obviously wasn't accustomed to being on the water. The bow of the boat seemed to move more than the rest, and he gripped the edge of the helm tighter each time the Boston Whaler plunged over the crest of a wave.

Without seeing the depth gauge, I judged the water to be about fifteen feet deep. It was harder to distinguish in rough conditions, but the color of the water was still pale blue. Luckily, the skies were clear, letting the sun shine bright.

A glance over my shoulder told me we were about two miles from shore. I saw the wave coming. It was a good six-foot swell, and the bow was aiming straight into it.

Water sloshed over the front as the Whaler climbed up the crest. The bow and midship cleared the water for a split second before gravity drove it down. I shifted my weight on my legs as I threw myself against Goon. He was still trying to get his stance stable from the jarring crash over the wave, and with both of our weights throwing us off center, he had no time to brace. He stumbled to the side, and I pushed harder, sending both of us over the gunwale into the sea.

We struck the water on our sides. As we sank, my left hand grabbed for the Glock. At the same time, I clawed at his throat. The water nullified his strength and size. Of course, it did the same to mine.

I wrenched the Glock from his hand. However, as he thrashed, I couldn't recover it. The gun sank to the bottom. My efforts refocused on subduing him, and I kicked my feet to drive us to the bottom.

I had the advantage of taking a deep breath before we hit the water, and I caught Goon offguard. At this point, it was about resiliency.

His hands tried to pound at me. It was the only defense he knew. Sheer force always worked for him, but underwater the blows were futile. He was only burning oxygen. I wrapped an arm around his throat, and he panicked as I tightened the grip.

Instinct caused him to claw desperately at my arm. I squeezed as his fingers pulled against my forearm. Now he was figuring out leverage was more effective than brute strength. However, he was burning out the oxygen as he continued to attempt to shake me off. My left hand jabbed at his eyes, causing him automatically to shield his face.

My own lungs burned, and I prayed he was exhausting himself faster than I was. All I had to do was hang on.

My gamble was that Goon would panic. Eventually, he'd inhale a lungful of water.

I felt it when he finally did. The fight in him intensified for a few seconds before the three-hundred-pound body went flaccid. I pushed Goon toward the bottom before kicking to the surface. My chest begged for a breath, but I paused as the ticking and whirring of the outboard moved away from me. They were circling, looking for us.

My head broke through the surface as I gasped for air. The waves lifted and lowered me as I treaded water. Berríos's boat was fifty yards away, making another pass on what they thought was their original path. The current and wind, though, carried both them and us away from each other.

They turned again. Berríos stood on the bow as the boat moved just over idle speed through the water. He raised his hand to his brow to block the sun as he peered across the waves, trying to find us.

When his head moved my direction, I sank below the surface for several seconds before coming back up. It wasn't likely he'd see me in these conditions. The sunlight would reflect off the waves, blinding him in the moments the waves lifted me up. When I fell back into a wave's trough, the crest would hide me.

For almost half an hour, I watched as the two men wandered in an ever-growing circle. The southern wind pushed the boat north while the loop current carried me south. The Boston Whaler finally adjusted its course toward shore and sped away. As far as the two men in the boat knew, Goon and I were lost causes at that point.

Once the fishing boat vanished in the distance, I started swimming for shore. Three miles wasn't a hard slog for me. While the surface conditions made it more difficult, I altered my strokes, so I wasn't fighting against the waves. There was little chance I'd win any medals, but I had no trouble covering three miles in a little over an hour.

As I approached the shore, I gauged the current had pushed me a couple of miles south. I focused on a sandy beach and kicked my feet. A few minutes later, the sandy bottom brushed against my legs, and I walked up onto the beach and collapsed on the sand.

After several minutes of lying in the sun, I sat up and fished the second phone Scar gave me out of my pocket. The salt water ensured it was useless.

I stood and looked both directions on the beach. It was empty. I'd walked ashore on the Shell Key Preserve–a small island separated by a small pass. With a sigh, I trudged north toward the pass connecting me to the closest road.

14

After three hours crossing the Shell Key Preserve and swimming another channel, I reached Pinellas Bayway and headed north toward St. Petersburg. The sun was drying my clothes, but it wasn't cleaning them. This was one of those times when I wanted at least a change of clothes.

My thumb came up as I hiked toward the St. Petersburg skyline. No one was going to stop for me, but it was the only thing I could do. The sea and sand don't bother me much. I live in it daily, but at least I keep a dry set of clothes on board to throw on while my others dry out.

As my feet shuffled along the asphalt, I lifted my eyes to stare across the bay. The sun was setting, and my body ached from the day. I needed to find some dry clothes and a bed. A cold beer would work wonders, too.

I wasn't sure what my next move was. Victor and Rosalina seemed off the radar for the moment. However, it didn't seem likely they could maintain that status for long unless they left the city. Eventually, they'd pop up. Everybody does. It's a human mistake. People get complacent. Moralez, or rather his people, would watch Rosalina's mother, expecting the girl to come home at some point.

A sign in the shape of a conch shell loomed ahead. Sea Shell Emporium promised a "wide range of shells and souvenirs." While the stated offerings were not great, I found a pair of board shorts and a plain t-shirt.

Sea Shell Emporium also offered snacks and drinks. I grabbed a twenty-four ounce bottle of water and a bag of pretzels. Behind the counter, a blond, blue-eyed high school kid manned the register. He gave me a strange look when I checked out. Although he was a teenager, so he probably judged everyone over the age of thirty. But I looked like a mess.

"Is there a hotel around here?" I asked.

"Yeah, down the road," he told me. "Maybe half a mile."

After thanking him, I hiked toward the motel. His estimation was off–I guessed it, closer to a little over a mile.

Once I got into a room, I tried the number for Scar's burner phone. No answer. I showered off the sand and salt before dropping onto the bed.

The next morning, I tried Scar's number again. Still no answer.

As I dressed, I thought about the photos of Victor I'd seen at his parents' home–particularly the one on the deck boat. It appeared to be the most recent one in his mother's house. The boat looked like a charter vessel, but the picture wasn't one a tourist would take. I'd had a hunch Victor was working on the boat when the photograph was taken.

I opened the bag of pretzels from the Shell Emporium as I dialed the number for a cab company. The taxi arrived

ten minutes later. I trashed the empty pretzel bag and
climbed into the back seat.

The driver took me on a ninety-three dollar ride to
the Marriott in downtown Tampa. I gave him a soggy
hundred-dollar bill as I climbed out.

From the Marriott, I could see two marinas. Both
stretched along the waterfront, and I couldn't remember
the angle the photographer took the picture. My gut told
me it was the one on the northern edge of the bay, so I
started there.

At the walkway, a tall white sign listed the charters at the
dock. I counted twelve in all. Every one appeared to be on
the front section closest to the shore.

Several slips were empty. I meandered past each one,
studying the boat as I attempted to match it to the
one in my memory. No doubt, I resembled the very
person most liveaboards despise–the lookie-loo. Those
people fascinated by boats troll up and down the marinas
examining each one. In fairness, it's the same thing one
might do if they were interested in buying a house, but the
difference is most of us consider our cockpits the same as
our living room. People strolling past us while we are on
our couches seem intrusive. It's our own fault, though,
for living lives outside the ordinary. Most people don't live
out in the open.

Still, here I was strolling along the dock, staring at each
vessel. I passed a scruffy man cleaning the deck around the
gangplank of an older flybridge sportfisher. He diverted
the nozzle of his power washer away from me.

I offered a gracious wave and signaled I wanted to ask him something. He released the trigger, letting the blast from the sprayer turn to a trickle.

"Sorry to bother you," I told him. "I'm looking for a guy who worked around here."

"Yeah," the dockworker responded, with some reservations. Most people looking for someone around here probably weren't coming around to catch up. Bill collectors and process servers made those kinds of rounds. This guy needed some incentive to help me.

"Yeah, this is the guy my sixteen-year-old sister has run off with. I'm just trying to find her," I lied.

He perked up a little, either from sympathy or empathy. Didn't matter. Both work. "Who is he?" he asked.

"Guy's name is Victor Berríos," I explained. "Might be a diver for one of the charters. He's about twenty. About my height, but skinnier."

He nodded but answered, "Never heard of him."

"Thanks," I responded, somewhat downtrodden.

"You might check with Carlos," he suggested.

"Who's Carlos?"

"He runs the dive charter down at the other end of the marina," he told me. "Got about three boats. He's worked with all the divers around here."

"Thank you," I acknowledged with a smile.

The man turned back to the deck, letting the jet of water wash the darkened wood until it showed streaks of bright yellow wood where the stream had torn away the discolored surface of the wood.

The dive charter was on the opposite end, and its name was missing on the big white board at the front. Dive Deep Charters took up a small section with several slips and a small building. A vertical air compressor stood next to a galvanized water trough. A rolling rack held various sizes of wetsuits and buoyancy compensators. I strolled past the two boats floating the slips. Either might be the vessel in the picture. The empty slip on the other side of the dock was positioned perfectly to capture the Marriott in the background.

As I pushed the door open, an electronic chime rang out across the water, alerting anyone nearby a customer was here.

A blond kid was cleaning masks and snorkels in a tub of soapy water. He glanced up at me.

"Hello," he greeted. "How can I help you?"

"You aren't Carlos, are you?" I asked, skeptical.

"No, sir," he responded with a grin. "Carlos is out on a charter. He should be back in the next few minutes. Can I help you?"

"I'm trying to find a man who worked for Carlos," I explained. "Victor Berríos?"

The kid gave me a puzzled stare. "I don't know him."

My lips pursed as I nodded. "You worked here long?" I asked.

"About six months," he told me.

"Guess I'll wait on Carlos," I replied. "If you don't mind."

"No, go right ahead," he answered.

"You been diving long?" I asked as I wandered around the shop.

"Since I was twelve," he said.

I didn't guess how many years that was. My initial instinct was to say six, but I was probably wrong.

The shop was a typical dive shop. Most of the gear seemed to be rentals. There were key chains and dive flag memorabilia with the Deep Dive Charters logo emblazoned on it. A rack of cheap Chinese masks were for sale at exorbitant prices.

Charts and maps covered one wall. Red ink marked the popular dive spots. Thumbtacks held pictures on the wall. Most were the same shot—a diver, whether male or female, in a half-stripped wetsuit holding a fish. Occasionally, there were groups of divers in wetsuits huddled together for a group picture. Everyone was smiling. It's hard to come out of the water after a dive without a grin, especially if you are bringing a speared bounty with you. Success breeds joy.

I paused in front of one picture. The image was of a grinning Victor Berríos with his arm wrapped around a young blond woman in a bikini. She held a speargun with a small barracuda hanging limply on the end.

The dock rumbled as an engine churned the water beneath it. After several seconds, the vibrations ceased. Excited voices sounded outside. The door opened, chiming to the marina, and two men pushed through the door like outlaws into a saloon. They each held their mask and fins over their right shoulder like they were a backpack.

"How was the dive?" the kid asked as they approached the desk.

"Great," one told him.

"We nailed a grouper," the other announced. "He got away."

"That happens," the kid acknowledged. "Lost a big one last week. Broke the line and took off with the spear straight through him."

Two women filed through the door, setting off the doorbell as they entered. They were intensely chatting to each other. Their fins and masks hung from each hand. The laughter they exchanged implied they enjoyed themselves.

As I said, it's hard not to smile after a dive.

"Mister," the kid called to me. "Carlos is outside if you want to talk to him."

It was a polite way to move me out of the cramped shop so he could tend to the actual customers. I took the hint and stepped outside.

Two bare-chested men were tying up the dive boat. The older one had dark hair with large streaks of gray. He wasn't all muscle, but he was still in shape. The other wasn't much older than the kid inside.

"Are you Carlos?" I asked the older man.

"Yeah," he responded, tying the last dock line around the cleat. "What can I do for you?"

"Listen, I know you just got back from a charter," I stated. "I'll make it quick. I'm looking for someone who probably worked for you."

The man straightened up. His dark skin wasn't all genetic. The years on the boat bronzed and leathered him. He appraised me for a minute before asking, "Who?"

"Victor Berríos."

Carlos lifted an eyebrow and continued to stare at me. "What are you wanting with him?" he questioned.

I considered the lie about my sister, but I thought better of it. Something told me this man sensed bullshit from a mile away.

"He's in some trouble," I explained. "He and his girlfriend are on the wrong side of some terrible people."

Carlos folded his arms across his bare torso. "How are you helping him?" he asked, warily.

"The girl is the daughter of a friend," I told him. "I want to get to them before someone else does."

The divemaster's eyes narrowed. "Someone else wouldn't be the shitheel of a father he had?"

"That would be one of them," I acknowledged.

"That kid came to work more than a few times with bruises," Carlos noted. "I threatened to have a one-on-one with the asshole, but Vic warned me his dad was connected. It wasn't worth it."

"The kid was right," I replied, thinking about my brief boat trip with the elder Berríos.

"What's he into?" Carlos inquired.

"My guess is it is a misguided attempt to get away from it all."

"Drugs?" he asked.

I nodded.

"That's why I had to let him go," Carlos explained. "He was taking the boat out on late night trips. Found a brick of what I guessed was coke on the boat. Figured he was smuggling it."

"Yeah," I nodded.

"The shitty part was I don't think he was using," the man told me. "I think he didn't have a choice."

"Well, when Dad is a runner for a big cartel," I confirmed. "Sometimes, you just do what it takes to survive."

Carlos shook his head. "I should have gone to the cops," he commented.

"That would only get you or him killed," I assured him. "These kinds of people don't mess around."

"What makes you think you can stop them?" he asked.

"Oh, I might not stop them," I responded. "I'll make them wish they hadn't tried, though."

Carlos shrugged. "I haven't got a clue where he is."

"When did you fire him?"

"Last July. Right before the Fourth."

I scratched my head, feeling sand mixed in my hair. "You don't know where he could have gone?" I asked. "Another charter company?"

"There are too many of them," Carlos answered. "I'd have no idea. It's not around here. I cross paths with most of the charters in the Bay."

He raised a finger, signaling me to wait as he shouted, "Jimmy, you know where Vic ended up working?"

The younger deckhand paused as he wound the loose lines on the dive boat into a coil. "Vic?" he repeated. He glanced around like we had caught him with his pants around his ankle.

Carlos goaded him. "C'mon, Jimmy. He's in a bit of trouble, it seems."

Jimmy responded, "He's running some guy's boat down south of here. Maybe around Naples."

"You know who the guy is?" I asked.

Jimmy just shrugged.

"Any chance you could see where he took the boat?" I asked Carlos. "I know my chart plotter will automatically track the GPS and store the waypoints."

The divemaster shook his head. "If I had it, it's all gone. We replaced the chart plotters a few months ago."

"Okay, thanks."

Carlos put his hands on his hips. "If you find him, tell him to get in touch with me," he said. "I want to help him if I can."

I nodded in appreciation.

15

This endeavor was costing me more than I bargained for when I left the Tilly. Between the motel room I found and the cab ride the next morning to where I left my rental car, I was out of cash. Luckily, I kept a secured credit card with a thousand-dollar balance for emergencies. I actually mean emergencies. Otherwise, I abhorred the thing. Part of my freedom requires me to be beholden to no one, including a bank that I owed nearly twenty-five percent interest.

I considered this one of those emergencies, unless I fancied walking seventy-five miles to the little topaz Versa parked in the convenience store lot where I left it. A piece of paper was under the right windshield wiper. The wind whipped the page, fluttering it until it appeared ready to fly away.

Scrawled handwriting covered the wind-whipped paper. It took a second to decipher the chicken scratch on the page. No signature–I guessed it was from Scar. "Toliver Bar and Grill. 10:00." At least, I thought it said "Toliver." It was nice of him to assume I escaped Berríos. There weren't a lot of options, I suppose. Once we slipped out the back, he'd just have to wait.

For a few seconds, I considered driving back to West Palm. Scar didn't ask for my help, and this was getting to be more than I wanted to deal with. Somehow, I kept thinking about Victor and Rosalina. Not that their actions were excusable.

My moral ambiguity about the drug trade clouded the issue. I didn't approve of dealing drugs. Most of the time, they ended up in the hands of people who didn't need them. Of course, the illegalization of them causes most of the violence. The so-called drug war our government has been fighting for the past forty years has only seen casualties with no victory. If Agent Kohl ever took Moreno down, it would be a matter of days before another filled the void. Within a month or two, business would be back up, and Kohl would have a new target.

If the era of Prohibition taught us anything, it should be that people are going to flock to the easiest fix they can get despite the laws preventing it. The United States could legalize it, regulate it, and tax it. Big business would step in, and the real criminals could get their hands on it. If Prohibition taught us anything–criminal activity will decrease.

I grew up in the wet county adjacent to several dry counties. Anyone from those other counties who wanted a twelve-pack of beer or a bottle of Jack Daniels had to drive across the county lines to find their drinks. Those same counties which outlawed alcohol had higher numbers of DUIs and alcohol-related deaths. The statistics spoke for themselves. The powers-that-be

enforced a moral imperative on the citizens, so those
constituents had to go elsewhere for their fix.

Unfortunately, morality laws were nothing new.
Lawmakers passed most as an effort to constrain certain
populations, whether based on age, sex, or gender. It
wasn't a problem I could ever solve.

Despite my aversion to Victor and Rosalina's course
of action, I knew what Victor was facing at home. He
just wanted an escape pod. Unfortunately, it would never
work for him. Men like Moralez feel no compassion or, at
least, didn't express it. That was bad for business.

Nonetheless, I felt for the young couple. There wasn't
much chance I'd head home just yet.

With several hours to kill, I drove inland until I found a
cheap motel, complete with a neon palm tree on the sign
and a small pool in the front. The Bayside Motel offered
a room which was a basic efficiency but still cost me $150.
At least it was quiet and mostly empty.

I shed my clothes and climbed into the shower to wash
off the salt on my skin. When I came out of the bathroom,
I dropped naked on top of the comforter. Within seconds,
I fell asleep.

My internal clock woke me four hours later. The only
light coming into my room shone from the street lamp in
the parking lot. With a stretch, I sat up and shook my head
to clear the sense of confusion one has upon waking.

The digital clock read 8:55 in red numbers. I flipped the
switch, illuminating the lamp on the bedside table.

By nine, I was locking the room behind me. The motel
clerk leaned back in his chair, watching some old movie.

I recognized Humphrey Bogart, but it wasn't one of the handful of his I knew. When I asked if he knew where the Toliver's Bar and Grill was, he regarded me with a scornful look, as if he knew something I didn't about the place. He grunted out some directions, but he had no idea what the address was.

When I pulled up to the bar, I realized the clerk might have been onto something. Even in thrift store shorts, I overdressed compared to the clientele. The bar was in the back of a somewhat crumbling structure. Calling it a building would offer it more credentials than it deserved. On the front side, someone secured a makeshift mechanic shop behind a double door made from two pieces of plywood. Presumably the mechanic was the one who spray-painted the word "Closed" across both pieces of wood, so that when the doors latched together, the entire word was readable. Old tires lined the front in stacks.

The inside of Toliver's wasn't much better. My feet stuck to the floor in places a mop hadn't seen in a decade. A layer of smoke lingered across the room. Colored lights splayed through the fog–a mixture of tobacco and cannabis. Several speakers blared the song of a woman lamenting about something in Spanish. My linguistic shortcomings left me to wonder what she was singing, but melancholy filled the tone.

Scar was not in sight. Given that the entire bar took up less than twelve hundred square feet, it would have been hard to miss him. I walked up to the bar and ordered a beer. The choice of beer was limited–Bud Lite, Sol, Cristal, and Bruja. I took a Sol.

The bartender was a short Latino man with a thin mustache and thick biceps. He sneered at me as I took my beer. Even the extra couple of bucks I left on the bar didn't affect him.

Behind the bar was a glowing Sol sign with a clock. I was still twenty minutes early, so I found an empty seat in the corner, allowing me to watch everyone.

There wasn't much point in rushing through the beer. It was only a few degrees below room temperature, and I doubted the little man put any on ice. At least, none he intended to offer the *gringo*. As I nursed the Sol, I watched the clock.

The man came in exactly five minutes until ten. It wasn't as brazen a variance as my presence–he was Latino. It was how he held himself. There was a sense of competence in his stride. He took half a second to scope the tables as he entered. His eyes never stopped on me, but he still noted where I was sitting.

He wasn't as big as the two goons were, but he was solid muscle. It would have been hard for most people to see the defined arm muscles under the black sport coat he wore over the polo shirt. The lines of musculature were barely visible along his neck. He worked to maintain the definition. In fact, he considered it more important than the actual strength training. It built in an intimidation factor. Probably why he wore the jacket over the short-sleeved shirt. When the time came to strike fear, he slipped the jacket off, revealing the sculpted arms. Most people would see the solid build and shrink back, fearing his strength.

There was no pretense in my demeanor. I studied him blatantly as he walked to the bar. He ordered a shot of tequila. The bartender pulled a bottle of Hornitos from under the bar and filled a glass halfway with it. He leaned against the bar casually, facing my direction. We spent several seconds in the path of each others' vision. The glass came up to his lips. His gaze seemed to be off into space, but he was actually staring at me.

He was here because of Scar. I only assumed it was Scar's handwriting. Perhaps, Mr. Tequila wrote the note, expecting to bring me here. He was alone. At least inside the bar. His backup might be outside, awaiting his call. I doubted it. While he wasn't trying to be obvious, he certainly wasn't hiding his intent. Had he brought a few guys in with him, it would have made little difference to him.

When I first entered, I counted the men in the room. Eleven men and three women, not counting Mr. Tequila. All spread out at the handful of tables and the bar. None of them acknowledged Mr. Tequila. However, I doubted I could count on them not to jump in if something started in here. I was the obvious outsider, and if mayhem broke out, people tend to defend the familiar. Mr. Tequila and I could go head-to-head without me feeling any trepidation. But twelve men against me would not end well for me.

When he finished his drink, he set the glass on the bar and moved toward me. His gait was slow and deliberate. I couldn't see a gun, but it made little sense for him to come at me unarmed.

He walked directly toward my table, pulled out the seat opposite me, and sat down.

I stared at him for a full second before commenting, "You could have brought me another beer from the bar."

Mr. Tequila offered me a wry half smile. "I don't think you'll be staying for another *cerveza*," he remarked with a Cuban accent.

I shrugged. "Never know. The atmosphere seems friendly here."

His grin didn't waver.

"We want the cocaine," he stated.

I made a show of glancing about with a faux look of confusion. "I don't know what you are talking about."

His bemused look remained plastered on his face. "If we don't get it back by tomorrow, Velasquez will die next. After that, the girl."

He didn't mention Victor, meaning the boy was already dead or had escaped.

"I don't know where Victor is," I told him, tossing aside any notion of naivete.

Mr. Tequila shook his head. "Victor won't do you any good. The goods he stole seem to be lost."

I nodded with realization. "You killed him before you found out where he hid it?"

He didn't respond.

I chuckled. "I guess the girl didn't know either. Makes sense. Victor hid it on his own."

Mr. Tequila never changed his expression.

"Boy, you guys are stupid. Was it his daddy? That man wasn't the smartest."

"You have until tomorrow to deliver the cocaine."

I shook my head. "What cocaine? You just said it was lost."

The man folded his thick arms and leaned back in the chair. He studied me before saying, "Julio Moreno can make restitution. Two hundred and fifty kilograms by tomorrow."

"You are shitting me, right?" I questioned. "I need a little more time than that."

"Tomorrow."

"You seriously think Moreno just keeps it lying around? He is as insulated as it comes. Plus, I'll have to drive back to Miami to get it. Give me two days."

Mr. Tequila cocked his head, locking eyes with me. "Two days. Not a second longer."

"If you hurt Velasquez, it will be war. Is that what Moralez wants?"

"It already is war," he told me as he stood. He turned and started away, repeating, "Two days."

I didn't move until the door to Toliver's closed behind him. Bounding to my feet, I followed him out the door. The street and sidewalk were both empty. My head rotated both directions in search of taillights.

None.

Mr. Tequila vanished.

16

Julio Moreno wasn't about to give me 250 kilograms of cocaine. I considered calling him to ask for it. However, I remembered Scar's comment that Moreno may want to keep clear to avoid a war, even if it meant Scar's life. I didn't want to find out how much Moreno actually valued Scar. Even pushing loyalty aside, it was another bit of poor business for a drug lord to allow another to extort him.

That didn't leave me a lot of options. I'd have to get Scar and Rosalina back without Moreno's help.

I needed Victor's stash of cocaine. The cocaine could only be lost if the young man was dead.

Of course, it might not be.

I considered what I asked Carlos about saved waypoints in the chart plotter. Victor was a skilled diver. According to Scar, Victor swept in and picked up the cocaine dropped by smugglers. It was common for drug runners to drop their cargo somewhere along the coast. The runners text the coordinates to someone else who can retrieve it. People are lazy, and as long as it's a suitable location, those drug runners probably used the same drop site a few times. If Victor had gone on a few pickups, it would be easy to beat them to the drop, hoist the dope off the seafloor, and scamper away.

An experienced diver might pick a familiar spot to hide it. If you are careful when choosing a location, the sea made the ultimate safe deposit box. I wouldn't want to leave it too long, though. Eventually, a storm might shift the sands or redefine the bottom, and the stash would wash away. Until that happened, one could make regular withdrawals from their own white coral garden.

After several intentional wrong turns and a long circuitous drive, I got back to the motel nearly certain no one followed me. The rush I received a couple of days ago when Tattoo and his friend first showed up had faded. It's funny how the human mind works. The adrenaline rush pulled me out of the months of funk I found myself in since I came back from Jamaica. For a bit, I just wanted to feel anything but the sense of loss. Even when one is self-aware enough to recognize the flaws in logic, the emotional roller coaster ride usually overrides that cognizance.

While Rosalina and Victor had mired themselves in their current predicament, something embedded this sense of responsibility in me. I didn't send Scar after them. Everyone made their own decisions. Most of those choices were morally questionable at best.

Still, I didn't think I could leave it alone.

Nor would Moralez and his men let me. They proved that the day the Goon Squad stepped up to my bar. I had a target on me, too. Even if the war between Moreno and Moralez could be avoided, I had no guarantee Moralez

wouldn't target me out of spite. My continued claims
I had no affiliation with Moreno would ensure I didn't
receive the protection he afforded his associates. Moralez
could send a new goon squad into the Manta Club one day
to pay me back for the trouble inflicted on him this week.

The prospect of continuously watching my back wasn't
something I wanted to have. It wouldn't be difficult for
me to pick up and leave. In fact, I could skip from island
to island for a few years, supplementing my income along
the way at various dive bars where tourists flock for fruity
drinks.

But I liked my life in West Palm Beach. If I didn't want
to deal with running away, I was stuck in this mire. At least
until I could navigate a clear path.

It was getting late, but I dialed a number on the motel
phone.

"Hello," Rob Isip answered.

"Rob, did I wake you?" I questioned apologetically.

"No, I was just watching Fallon."

"Can I interest you in a trade?"

"What do you have to trade?" he asked shrewdly.

Rob was a lieutenant in the Coast Guard, pulling desk
duty in Fort Lauderdale. After we first met, I took Rob
and his wife, Tricia, on a weekend cruise. Since then,
Tricia has been hounding him about getting a boat for
themselves. I've helped him stave off her desire with several
trips around the coast.

"Two weeks to Andros," I suggested. "Some diving and
snorkeling along the way."

"You know, this would work better with Tricia," he replied.

"Oh, I meant for her," I quipped. "I suppose you can come too."

He chuckled, and he covered the phone to say something to his wife.

"Yes!" she shouted to me. "Whatever you want, Chase!"

Rob spoke again. "Sounds like you got a deal," he conceded. "What are you into?"

"Something ugly," I told him. "I have an acquaintance mixed up with a drug dealer."

"Geez, Chase," he remarked. "Some of your friends make bad choices."

"He's not a friend," I told him. "Just a victim of terrible circumstances."

I didn't figure Rob wanted to know how embedded I currently was between Moreno and Moralez. The Coast Guard spends a lot of time and energy intercepting drug smugglers. Until I was free and clear of this mess, I didn't want to bring anything down around me.

"What can I do?" he asked.

"I think he's hiding on a boat," I explained. "He was staying at a guy's house. Same guy might own a boat too."

"Hmm," Rob mused. "What's the name?"

"Carl Oxenwise," I told him.

It might have been a stretch, but if Oxenwise was in business with Victor, it might make sense the drug dealing wasn't the only occupation the two men shared. Jimmy, the mate on the dive boat, thought Victor was running a boat somewhere. I've found most people's lives aren't as complicated as they seem. Humans develop habits, liking familiar surroundings. That includes friends. I could be wrong, but from my perspective, Oxenwise was as good a prospect as any–plus I knew his name.

"I'll look in the morning," Rob promised me. "Can I call you back at this number?"

I had nowhere to go yet. "Yeah, I'll be here in the morning."

"If you don't hear from me, call me after lunch."

I didn't want to tell Rob I was in a time crunch. It may or may not matter. So, I replied, "Will do."

I heard him talking to Tricia. "Chase," he commented, "Trish wants to know when."

"I need a week to get things settled. Tell her end of the month. I need to get back on the water."

Tricia shouted, "Chase, you better bring your earplugs!"

I laughed as I hung up the phone.

As I lay back on the bed, I wondered how they grabbed Scar. Even if someone tried to snare him, I imagined the fight would be ugly, leaving at least someone maimed or dead. Normally, it would take meticulous planning to get the drop on him. Of course, we are all human. One's own ego can foul the best operational security.

Out of curiosity, I dialed the number for Scar's burner phone. No ringing. Just straight to a recording telling me to leave a message.

I sighed and leaned back on the bed. For the first time in a long while, loneliness washed over me. I'd spent a great deal of time alone and was rarely lonely.

This wasn't some sadness over Scar or even his daughter.

It was the exhaustion one has after losing someone. Or a few someones.

Death is far from new to me. I'd seen men die. Some were friends. Almost family. Others I've killed. Some died because of me. Those are the ones I can't stop feeling.

I studied the ceiling for several minutes before closing my eyes.

When the phone rang, I jerked up. Daylight was streaming through the slit between the curtains. Still on my back, I hadn't moved an inch in at least eight hours.

"I got what you want, Chase," Rob told me through the phone.

Still groggy, I mumbled something.

"There's a forty-two foot 1984 Chris Craft Catalina registered to Carl Oxenwise. He registered the boat out of Boca Grande."

"Thanks, Rob," I muttered.

"Keep your head down, man," he urged me before hanging up.

17

Boca Grande was a little less than a two-hour drive south. A dark cloud moved across the water to the west, preparing to drop a mid-day rainstorm on the area. It would come in with a deluge, but pass within a few hours.

Oxenwise kept his boat at the Boca Harbor Marina. As I pulled up to the marina, I studied the six rows of docks. Like most, the management segregated the sailboats to a different finger. Easy to eliminate those. The smaller boats lined the southern edge. The marina's designers may figure they could handle the southwest wind pushing them around more than some of the bigger vessels.

Unlike the marina in Tampa, Boca Harbor appeared to be almost all pleasure craft. The few liveaboard vessels were obvious—they wore a lived-in appearance with packed decks. Most weekend boaters stow their gear before jetting off home. Those of us that are permanent residents do like everyone in a house does. We procrastinate.

Of course, I say "we" only because I am a liveaboard. I'm also a stickler for keeping *Carina's* decks clear. I carry a few water toys like a kayak, but they remain secured in place. However, there's a reason so many look down on the liveaboard lifestyle. It can get messy.

Once I eliminated the sailboats and the smaller vessels, I had four fingers jutting out into the harbor. I picked the one on the southern side.

Rob didn't give me the name of the boat, so it relegated me to identifying the Chris Craft on sight. It wasn't an uncommon vessel on the water, but most of the ones I'd seen were older, like Oxenwise's.

There are several common divides among boat people. It starts with cruisers and day-sailors. Weekenders and liveaboards. Sailboats and powerboats. Outboards and inboards. The biggest divide was the gotta-have-a-new-boat and the old-boats-last-forever group. It's an unspoken rivalry in which both sides stare at the other, wondering how they manage it.

I fall in the old-boats category. Not that *Carina* was as old as some yachts are. She was an '86 model which made her over thirty years old and just a couple of years younger than Oxenwise's yacht. However, those fiberglass models can last forever with proper care. *Carina's* previous owner completely refitted the interior, so she was like brand new.

A lot of the new-boat crew think all older boats are derelicts, just waiting to sink. Since I, as well as the prior captain, performed constant maintenance, my baby still sailed better than any off-the-factory-floor model.

The marina ran about half and half of old versus new. They were mixed in fairly evenly, so I trudged along the dock, studying each one.

The Chris Craft was a fly bridge model with a small aft deck. Most of the space was in the cabin, so it didn't have the deck space some of the newer models had.

When I spotted her across the marina, I saw someone addressed the lack of deck area by adding a sizable swim platform to her stern. Blue letters scrawled across the back in a bubble font that read, *Going Down*. Boaters and their double entendres.

As I walked back up the dock to move across to the other finger, I passed a woman reclining on a folding lounge chair. She made a motion of lowering her sunglasses to examine me as I walked past. The evidence of cosmetic work was barely noticeable. Her doctor was skilled. But the lips always seem to give it away. The hair color was a shade too red to match her skin tone. Someone with that color hair wouldn't bronze the way she had.

Her husband or companion was on top of the Carver yacht, washing the forward deck with a power washer.

She offered a slight smile, to which I nodded with a half-smile. Her fingers dropped the glasses back onto the bridge of her nose as if she'd finished her appraisal of me.

I turned my head with a smile as I passed. Her expression didn't crack, but her fingers drummed the side of her sunglasses.

Going Down fit one of the more worn old-boat categories. Scuffs and scratches marked the hull with years of rubbing against docks and piers.

I wasted no time climbing aboard. Most marina people barely know the people a few slips down unless they are all liveaboards.

The bikinied ginger in sunglasses wasn't a liveaboard. If the boat wasn't enough of a clue, the intricately pedicured toes didn't belong to someone who spent all day climbing around on a boat. I guessed she was far enough down the dock to ignore Oxenwise and his weathered vessel.

The hatch was secured. Like most of the locks securing boats, this one wasn't much more than a small padlock secured by a two-inch hasp held into the fiberglass by two quarter-inch screws. It was enough to deter some, but when I jerked the padlock down, the two brass screws bent with a snap as they tore out of the side.

The motion was quicker than using a key, and I didn't waste the time to look around for any witnesses. After all, I belonged here. People who belong don't appear suspicious.

The Chris Craft was definitely being used as a dive charter. Three wet suits hung around the salon with various regulators. Several cylinders were strapped into a homemade tank holder attached to the starboard side.

There weren't a lot of personal touches to the boat. No knick knacks or cutesy nautical themed gear. It felt like a business more than a pleasure boat.

Water, beer, and easy-to-eat snacks, perfect post-dive nutrients, stocked the galley. I pulled a bottled water from the fridge and opened it. As I drank it down, I moved down the steps to the forward cabin.

The berth was disheveled. Someone had been sleeping on it, but the room didn't feel lived in. It was more of a crash-pad. Or someplace someone was hiding. Either way, the last tenant wasn't here.

I moved the sheets and blankets, searching for anything showing Victor and Rosalina had been here. Nothing definitive reared its head.

The hanging closet only held masks and fins. After rifling through the drawers to find only towels and extra t-shirts, I moved up to the bridge.

A few years back, a former Marine buddy of mine got entangled in some messy things. In fact, it was because of Tristan it occurred to me to check the chart plotter. Tristan marked several locations he used to hide some of his ill-gotten gains.

On the bridge, I powered up the Garmin chart plotter. The map appeared showing the little triangle that designated *Going Down*. As I scrolled through the menu, I searched for saved waypoints. There were none.

I leaned back in the captain's chair, staring out the forward windows. My attention returned to the plotter, and I found the history. The chart plotter installed on *Carina* tracked my course. I liked to look back and see how circuitous my sailing course is. When one depended on the wind to guide him, the course might meander all directions to get to the final destination.

This device did the same thing. The memory only included the last thirty trips. At thirty-one, it overwrote the earliest ones unless the user changed the settings.

Oxenwise hadn't done that. I flipped through the last six trips. Four of them went to the same coordinates–twenty miles off shore. The depth was between forty-five and fifty feet. The vessel appeared to remain at that spot for over an hour before heading back to the marina.

It could be a dive spot. Most charts noted wrecks and reefs, and there were no markings at this location. When I scrolled back through the rest of the history, I found several runs to different spots. Many of those were marked with either a CO or fish bones, designating them as reefs or wrecks.

I zoomed in on the first spot in the chart plotter's history without any chart markings. Nothing denoted anything of interest here. It didn't mean it couldn't be a place only the divemaster knew about, but it seemed unlikely.

The only way to know for sure was to go out there. I'd already broken into the boat. What was stopping me from borrowing it for a few hours? Oxenwise was still in the hospital.

It took three minutes to find the ignition key. It was in an unlocked cash-box under the sink. The two Crusader engines rumbled to life, and I made my way around the vessel, releasing all the dock lines.

My hand pressed the dual throttle controls down, and the Chris Craft pulled out of the slip. As soon as the stern cleared the slip, I reversed the port engine, spinning the vessel almost ninety degrees. Before it over-rotated, I shoved the controls forward. The sixteen-ton yacht moved out of the marina.

Once I cleared the first navigational buoy, I increased the RPMs and sped the vessel up slowly. By the time I passed the next marker, I was planing out.

I set the autopilot to take me toward the coordinates on the chart plotter. The sea was churning as the storm I'd seen off shore earlier moved quickly toward me.

In minutes, sheets of rain blurred all visibility. The radar was binging as it pinpointed several other ships in my vicinity. My course took me between them all with room to spare. I stayed on guard for the next half-hour as *Going Down* climbed over the swells the wind threw at her. The ride on *Carina* would have been bouncy. Her narrower beam allowed the waves to roll her around like a pinball.

As I suspected, the storm passed over me in less than forty-five minutes. The sun ripped the clouds apart once the ominous majority reached shore. I straightened up to stare in awe as the waves calmed after the storm.

As the little triangle that represented *Going Down* neared the coordinates, I slowed the engines. On the eastern horizon, I saw the faint outline of the shore. Every other direction was nothing but water. Far to the north, I spotted a silver flash that came from a vessel heading back to land.

The depth gauge registered forty-three feet. Oxenwise had the controls for the anchor windlass on the helm. I dropped the anchor, listening to the clank-clank-clank as the chain fed out of the anchor locker. The digital readout told me I'd dropped a hundred feet of chain. If I planned to stay too long, I'd let the scope out twice that much. Instead, I let another fifty feet out before I stopped the windlass. I wasn't sure how much chain Oxenwise had, and the last thing I wanted was the bitter end to feed out into the Gulf.

Both engines turned silent when I cut the key. Small waves splashed against the hull, creating the only sound. The little triangle drifted south on the chart plotter as the current carried me away from the anchor. After a few seconds, the chain groaned as it stretched. The anchor stuck, and the little triangle stopped moving.

I climbed down and pulled out the scuba gear I'd found. After a quick check, I found all the cylinders were full. I could spend the rest of the afternoon diving around down here. Hopefully, I wouldn't need to do that.

After spreading all the gear out, I found a wet suit and selected a buoyancy compensator device, or BCD, in my size. The only thing I couldn't find was a weight belt. Normally, I would add ten pounds to help push me down faster. I've often joked that I was extra buoyant because my father was so full of hot air. Whatever the cause, I would have to work a little harder to get down. It wasn't an ordeal, just an annoyance.

I stared across the waves as I pulled the BCD over my chest. After adjusting the mask around my eyes and nose, I dropped into the water.

18

My skin prickled as the cold water filled my wetsuit. The first couple of seconds are usually chilly, even in a Neoprene suit. The water has to get between the skin and rubber material. Once it does, the body heats the liquid until the temperature becomes comfortable or, at least, tolerable.

It was better than my bare-skinned swim yesterday. Without some added weight, the rubber in the wetsuit would cause me to float more than I normally did.

I stroked toward the bow of the boat. When I reached the front, my hands caught the chain. The regulator slipped into my mouth, and I dumped any air I had in my BCD. I inverted head down and climbed down the rode toward the bottom. The forty-pound anchor would assist me in reaching the bottom, but once I reached the sea floor, I'd have to fight to stay down.

Since the storm ended, the sun was beaming through the water, and while the waves disrupted the light, the rays still gave me thirty feet or more of visibility. More, I wagered, considering I could make out the white sandy seafloor. As I kicked my feet and pulled my body deeper, the contours of the ocean floor appeared as ridges and waves of sand.

My right elbow wrapped around the chain long enough for me to clear my ears as the pressure increased in my sinus cavities and eardrums. The familiar sensation always made me think I'd heard a pop that never happened.

I continued deeper. The anchor sank into the sand around forty-three feet, give or take a foot. I'd have plenty of time to search around.

The bottom of this section of the Gulf appeared barren. Only a few tiny fish skimmed across the sand, searching for nibbles in the grains. As I twisted around, I surveyed the bottom. As far as I could see, the seafloor resembled a desert. No rocks, corals, or even trash to act as fish havens.

It also meant there didn't appear to be anything unusual here.

As soon as I let go of the anchor rode, the wetsuit lifted me a foot off the bottom. I pedaled my feet and swam with my arms to keep myself within a foot of the seafloor.

The emptiness left me with a brick in my gut. My hunch could be wrong.

I had plenty of air, so I started a search pattern. The depth gauge had a small, luminescent compass on the back. The anchor needed to be the center of my search. I swam north for about a hundred feet.

My fingers scraped across the sand as I counted out the distance. Somehow, distance is hard to estimate under water. I assume the effect results from the light distortion below the surface, but I've never researched the cause. It might just be me. Whatever the reason, I used my body length to count out approximately one hundred feet. My estimation was probably a few feet short.

I wished I'd carried something to mark the edge of my search radius. Futilely, I swiped a large X in the sand, knowing the mark would likely be gone if I made a complete circle. I turned south to locate the anchor. It was just out of my visibility.

I jostled between swimming south east, or returning to the anchor. The safest thing would be to make my way back to my starting point. With no reference points, it would be easy to get several hundred yards off course. I might end up getting lost and surfacing to find I'd meandered half a mile away from the boat. That's if I was lucky. With a full tank, I could cover a couple of miles without blinking.

A medium-sized grouper ambled past to my right. I paused, watching him glide along with no cares about me.

With my compass, I took another reading to verify my location before I followed my whim and swam after the fish. He paid me zero attention as he continued southeast.

The chalky box came into view. At first, I saw nothing more than a mound, but the angular edges bore a striking difference to the flat bottom. Like a new patch of white coral, the mere existence of the foreign object attracted the curiosity of smaller fish. In turn, larger predators like the grouper would swoop in for a bite.

As I approached the container, I realized the shape was an oversized cooler, the watertight kind designed to hold ice for weeks. Easily a six-hundred-dollar cooler at an REI or West Marine. Several needlefish darted away as I reached for the cooler. With a tug, I dragged the box several feet before realizing something secured it to the ocean floor.

My hands brushed away a stainless-steel chain with a padlock securing it to a buried pipe. The sixteen-inch diameter pipe measured about six feet long and seemed full of concrete. No amount of heaving I did would move it more than a few inches at a time.

My air would run out long before I inched the box over to the anchor. If I opened the lid under water, whatever was inside might be ruined. While I assumed it was the cocaine everyone was searching for, I didn't need it scattered into the surrounding water.

For a second, I wondered what effect it might have on the sea life. The parts per million had to be fairly low even with that much coke. I shook the thought away as I took another heading and swam toward the anchor. The trek back was slow as I counted off the feet between the anchor and the cooler.

My arms and legs were tiring as I fought to stay close to the bottom. After I started toward the surface, I relaxed, holding the rode loose to guide me toward the boat.

When my head broke through the water, I found I had plenty of air still. I inflated the BCD so I could slip out of it and secure it to the swim platform before I climbed aboard.

Going Down had a davit on the port side for lifting a dinghy up out of the water. I checked the cable. There wasn't enough to feed it all the way to the bottom, but it took less than two minutes of searching to turn up a hundred feet of coiled line–plenty of rope to pull the cooler aboard. All I needed was to cut the chain.

It took longer to find something for that task. Finally, I came across a small hacksaw in the engine compartment. Oxenwise or someone hadn't put it away, and the tool remained almost completely hidden under a hose.

The blade was old and rusty, but it should do the job.

I found a granola bar in the galley and ate it with a bottle of water before going back into the water. Once I reached the anchor, it took me two minutes to make my way back to the box. The needlefish returned in my absence. The grouper didn't make another appearance. Guess he grabbed something and moved along.

This swim was more of a struggle than the first. The coiled rope over my shoulder hampered the mobility of my right arm, but I stayed near the ocean floor.

My old saw blade made little impact on the thick links of the chain, and after a minute of grinding on them, I surrendered. Even with a close inspection, the cut in the chain was barely noticeable.

My attention turned to the padlock. It wasn't an ideal choice for the salt water environment. While it was still new, the short time the lock was under water showed small dots of rust on the metal. Three minutes of sawing broke the old blade. The fissure was almost through the shackle. I dropped the hacksaw, and using both hands, I twisted the lock in different directions. Once I felt the wiggle as the metal gave way, I continued to twist and turn the lock. It finally snapped loose, and I pulled the chain off the cooler.

Even free, the contents weighed a significant amount. With the end of the coiled line, I tied a half hitch and two round knots around the handle.

After uncoiling the line, I swam for the anchor. One hand guided me along the anchor chain to the surface while the other held the loose end of rope.

As soon as I reached the swim platform, I secured the loose end to a cleat and climbed aboard.

Before I tied off the line to the davit, I pulled the BCD and cylinder onto the aft deck. I leaned against the rail and stared across the water. There were still no other vessels in sight. It was a smart ploy. This stretch of water didn't offer any natural reefs, and I guessed there were few artificial ones, but overall, the fishermen found little worth in dropping hooks out here.

As the winch whined and whirred, the line wound around the reel and fed onto the deck. There was too much rope to wind it around the winch drum, so I removed the cable and rigged it to pull the line around the drum and as long as I continued to pull pressure against it, the rope came out smoothly.

It was a slow task, and by the time the cooler broke through the surface, my already-tired arms were aching from the perpetual motion.

The cooler bounced against the hull, and I climbed onto the swim platform to drag it out of the waves.

After releasing the latches, I opened the lid to find stacks of tightly wrapped white bricks. My fingers peeled the plastic away until the white powder crumbled on the tips.

I couldn't tell cocaine from chalk, but I assumed this must be Moralez's stolen stuff. I wrapped the brick back up.

Instead of attempting to heave the cooler up the ladder, I tossed the individual bricks up on the aft deck. Once the cooler was lighter, I hoisted it up to the rail over my head.

Once I climbed up after it, I stared at the pile of bricks, wondering what I was going to do next.

If I called or, rather, waited for his man to call, it likely wouldn't matter if I returned the drugs. In fact, I might put myself more firmly in the crosshairs. Either way it went, Rosalina and her father would be nothing more than liabilities.

The one thing I knew was it didn't need to stay where it was. If Oxenwise or Rosalina knew the location, it might not take long to drag it out of them. It couldn't stay on *Going Down* either. If I found the boat, so could someone else.

I needed to move it.

Once the anchor broke free, I motored southeast toward the coast. While the autopilot carried me on my heading, I stashed the loose bricks back into the cooler.

Half an hour later, I dropped the cooler back into about eighteen feet of water. Oxenwise kept an extra stern anchor in one of the rear lockers. After securing the anchor to it, I attached a round fender to mark the location.

I was risking a random fisherman coming along, thinking he'd scored a new bumper, but I hoped it wouldn't stay here over twenty-four hours. It would make retrieving it a lot simpler if I didn't need to dive to find it again.

Once I felt comfortable with where I left it, I committed the coordinates to memory. No point leaving any clues for anyone else.

I pointed the bow towards Boca Grande. As I motored back, I cleared the history on the chart plotter. No point leaving any trails.

By the time I reached the motel, it was after dark. I left *Going Down* in the same condition I'd initially borrowed her–minus three bottles of water, two granola bars, and half a cylinder of air.

When I pulled into the motel lot, I had a bag of fast-food tacos and a six-pack of Jai Alai. Both of which remained in my passenger seat when my driver's door opened and the cold barrel of a Glock pressed against my face.

19

"Get out!" a voice in the dark demanded.

My hands lifted as I twisted to get out of the rental. Thick fingers wrapped around my shirt and jerked me free of the car. I stumbled, and the hand shoved me to the ground.

"You're some kind of soldier, *verdad*?" the same voice hissed as someone pressed a foot against the back of my shoulder.

The asphalt, still hot from the Florida sun, pressed against my skin. The aroma of hot tar filled my nostrils.

"Not so tough now?" the man mocked, pressing the barrel against the base of my skull.

"What do you want?" I questioned. The foot pushing me into the pavement muffled my voice.

"Which room is yours?" he demanded.

I didn't answer. Nothing I said could help me. If they planned to kill me, taking me to my room only provided them some cover. At least here in the parking lot, there might be witnesses.

From my position on the blacktop, I counted six shoes, plus the foot pressed against my head probably had a match. Four guys. Four very careful guys.

They murmured to each other in Spanish. Nothing I could make out, though.

When I didn't respond, the same hand that jerked me out of my seat searched through my pockets.

"¡Aqui!" he exclaimed, pulling the room key from my back pocket.

Four hands now grabbed me by the arms and pulled me up. My face stung as the initial jerk scraped the pavement with my cheek.

Once on my feet, I took several seconds to study the four faces. I recognized one as the boat driver. The other three were new to me.

"Vamos," the one with the Glock 9 mm ordered, pointing toward room 126 after he read the number scrawled in Sharpie on the key tag. His face wasn't quite misshapen, but it was obvious his nose was once broken. He had a few scars peppering his cheek, the telltale scars of shrapnel. He had a milder case than any I'd seen before. Whatever exploded had at least only caused him minimal damage.

The two men gripping my arms held me tight. They didn't want to give me an inch to react. Both could have been clones of the two goons I'd already killed. Although, these two each had distinctive ink marking them. One had a scrawling tattoo around his throat. The other had an unusual symbol that resembled a monkey sitting with something hoisted on his shoulders. The primate's genitals were clearly identifiable. An interesting choice for a face tattoo.

"Bring the soldier-boy," Shrapnel Face demanded, stomping toward the motel.

Throat Tattoo and Monkey Face practically lifted me up, pushing me behind Shrapnel and the boat driver. Shrapnel let himself into my room and sat down on the chair. The boat driver scanned the room, likely looking for any weapons I might have stashed. He gave a nod to Shrapnel, who pointed toward the bed.

Monkey Face let go of my arm long enough to hit me in the face twice. My face swelled and a warm trickle of blood dripped out of my nose. Throat Tattoo took several punches into my gut, bending me over. Another blow hit my face, and I lost count as the two thugs belted me with blows.

I teetered and fell over on the bed.

"Enough," Shrapnel announced.

My face throbbed, and I wheezed through my broken nose.

"Are you ready to talk, Soldier?"

I lifted my head to stare at Shrapnel. After sucking in a deep breath, I pushed myself up into a sitting position.

"Marine," I rasped.

"*¿Que?*" Shrapnel asked.

"Not a soldier," I stated in a low, threatening tone. "I'm a fucking Marine."

He smirked and shifted his eyes to Throat Tattoo. He hit me in the face again, knocking me to the side.

"Anything else to say?" Shrapnel questioned.

For the second time, I pushed myself back into a sitting position. There wasn't much chance I'd give him too much satisfaction, but it seemed the better part of valor was to survive the next bit.

Shrapnel pulled out a phone and pressed a few buttons. I heard a ding, and Shrapnel turned the phone to face me. The screen showed an older Latino man in his fifties staring at the screen.

"Gordon?" he questioned, squinting his eyes as he studied me.

"And you are?" I mumbled through my swollen lips.

"I'm Juan Moralez," the man introduced himself. "You've become something of a thorn in my side."

I spat a clump of blood out. "In my defense, your guys dragged me into it. I was minding my business."

"It seems you've ignored my message from last night," the drug lord commented.

I nodded, responding, "It's pointless. I have nothing to do with this. Your man even said the cocaine was lost."

"You're working for Moreno," he argued. "If he wants to prevent more bloodshed, he can provide what he has stolen."

"That makes little sense," I replied. "First, I'm not working for anyone. I'm a damned bartender. Second, you want someone else to repay you for something you lost. That's just sloppy business."

"I don't believe you," he refuted. "I've lost several men to you. It seems you are Moreno's secret weapon."

"That's insane," I told him.

The man ignored me. "If you expect to see your friend, Velasquez, alive, I expect you to bring my cocaine to me."

"The cocaine your man's kid stole?" I questioned, trying to lift an eyebrow. The swelling in my face was limiting my facial expressions.

"With the help of Velasquez," he told me.

"That's bullshit," I said in a flat tone. "Velasquez had nothing to do with it."

"Gaspar, kill him," Moralez ordered. "He seems to be of no help."

Shrapnel raised the barrel of the Glock toward me.

"Whoa! Whoa! Whoa!" I shouted, raising my hand. "Let's slow down a bit."

"Why, Mr. Gordon?" Moralez asked. "You just told me you couldn't help me."

"Look, this is getting out of hand," I blathered. "I don't work for Moreno, I promise that. But I can do something. I don't work for him, but I can reach out to him."

"*Esperas,* Gaspar, *"* Moralez interjected. "Mr. Gordon, you need to decide."

"Fine, Juan," I sneered. "I'll get you your cocaine. But I'm going to need some extra time."

"No," he denied.

"Seriously, Juan," I began, but Throat interrupted my sentence when he struck me again.

Shrapnel, or Gaspar, ordered, "You will call him *Señor* Moralez or Mr. Moralez. Not Juan."

I gave a curt nod. My head was swirling now, and I was struggling to concentrate.

Moralez began talking again. "Tomorrow, Mr. Gordon. Otherwise, I will slice *Señor* Velasquez into little pieces and use him as bait."

The drug lord's face disappeared as the screen changed. He panned his camera around a room until it stopped on the bloodied face of Scar. The enforcer was bound to a chair with thick plastic zip ties. The blood-caked face looked worse than mine felt–a feat I didn't think possible over the last few moments. On the floor behind him was a young woman wearing only a torn shirt. She cowered in a ball, waiting for whatever torture was coming next.

Scar focused his eyes on me. Rage burned in his pupils, but I saw in his countenance a plea for help. It wasn't for himself. I knew men like Velasquez. His life had been on a razor's edge for as long as he could remember. Likely longer than I thought possible.

No, that desperation was for Rosalina.

My imagination didn't need to be vivid to guess what she'd endured. She paid for the sins of her father, Victor, the senior Berríos, and who-knows-who. Maybe even my shortcomings.

Now, I heard the unspoken begging of a man who had never pleaded for anything. All I could offer was a small, nearly imperceptible nod.

He blinked back at me.

I told Jay the other day that Scar was a man I couldn't help respecting. He was a different kind of warrior, and while I didn't agree with everything he fought for, he had a level of honor. At least, I perceived it. If I found he'd tortured a young woman, the way Moralez did Rosalina, I'd not hesitate a second before putting a bullet between his eyes. I felt Moreno too had a certain level of ethical criminality. Certain actions were unforgivable.

Moralez didn't have the same compunction. It would be his undoing. He'd crossed a line, and he expected no one to push back. He was nothing more than a despot, ruling with an iron fist. Like so many before him, ruling during prosperity was easy. It was only tested during days of starvation.

I cleared my throat, swallowing some blood. "I'll get it for you," I promised.

"Good," Moralez replied, turning the camera back to his face. The smirk on his face was more than self-satisfied. He felt he had won this tête-à-tête. "You have until tomorrow."

"Where do you want me to bring it?" I asked.

Moralez grinned at me as if I made some childish mistake. "I'll have Gaspar find you tomorrow. If you decide to hide, then I'd suggest you remain hidden."

I stared at the screen, trying to decide if I was going to kill him or not.

The picture went blank, and Gaspar pocketed the phone.

"I'll be seeing you tomorrow," Gaspar paused before adding, "Marine."

"Careful," I muttered. "I've made tougher men than you four eat those words."

Gaspar grinned at me. Something in the pit of my stomach told me he had a sadistic nature. This wasn't simply work. It was in his eyes. "Tomorrow," he hissed.

The four men left the room, leaving the door ajar.

"My key," I whispered, realizing Gaspar still had it. It was an unspoken threat—try to sleep knowing that they could come back with no notice. I pushed up to my feet and stumbled toward the door.

As I pushed it closed, I heard a crash of broken glass. Gaspar stood at my rental car with a lascivious smile. Glass shards sprinkled on the ground around the Cuban's feet as he shattered the window. He moved around the car, smashing the windows with the butt of his Glock.

"I hope you cut your hand," I mumbled, keeping my eyes on the four of them as they climbed into a blue GMC Enclave.

The boat driver seemed relegated to chauffeuring everyone, and he gunned the engine as he pulled out of the lot.

When the SUV was out of sight, I grabbed the ice bucket and shuffled down to the ice machine. After returning to my room, I dumped the contents onto a towel I spread on the bed. I dropped onto the bed and placed the folded ice pack on my face.

Moralez didn't just want his cocaine. He wanted me to start a war. He intended to take a pound of flesh from Moreno. Either the man conceded and gave Moralez the coke he was demanding or Moralez killed his lieutenant. Whatever happened would be a mark on Moreno. That wouldn't be the end of it either.

My eyes closed, letting the cold ease the pain in my face. I wasn't sure what to do next.

The coke's new location was mine alone. But it wasn't an issue of handing it over to him. Moralez had no intention of letting Scar or Rosalina go free. Right now, they were nothing more than pawns to trade. Something with which to manipulate me and Julio Moreno.

After I'd lain there for half an hour, the ice left my face numb and swollen. It wasn't helping, and I didn't enjoy sitting still.

The towel, propelled by my frustration, flew across the room. The last bits of melting ice spilled onto the dingy carpet.

I needed to do something. The last thing I could do was play this out the way Moralez wanted.

20

The room was no longer safe. It wouldn't have surprised me if Gaspar left Throat Tattoo or Monkey Face to watch the motel. No doubt planning to follow me. Why bother waiting for me to deliver the cocaine if they could kill me and steal it? Moralez may have thought I'd lead him to an opening to take on Moreno.

Of course, none of that was going to happen.

I grabbed the phone. If I only planned to spend a few more minutes here, it didn't matter who I called. Let the feds trace the number back here. I planned to be gone in the next ten minutes.

The digital clock beside the phone said it was only a few minutes past eight. Still early enough.

The other line rang.

"Padrino's," a youthful, feminine voice answered.

"Is Julio Moreno in?" I asked.

The girl on the other end responded, "There is no one here by that name."

"It's important you deliver a message for me," I told her.

"Um…"

"Tell him Chase Gordon needs to talk to him immediately." I rattled off the motel's number and my room extension before hanging up.

It was more than likely Agent Kohl's team tapped the phone line at Padrino's, but Julio would call back on a safe number. While I waited, I moved to the bathroom mirror, where I stared at the damage Throat and Monkey did. They broke my nose. Not the first time it happened, though. I ground my teeth together as I put an index finger on either side and pushed it straight. An excruciating pain shot from the bridge of my nose through my skull. The only sound I let out was a deep grunt.

I reexamined my handiwork. It wasn't as crooked, but it hadn't been straight since a bar fight during a weekend furlough from Parris Island.

After soaking a washcloth in hot water, I cleaned the blood off my face. My right cheek had a two-inch gash. It needed a stitch or two, but there wasn't enough time. I'd find a Walgreens and do some maintenance soon.

My left eye had a slight cut and bruising formed around it. By tomorrow, it would be a nice shiner. Throat also split both my upper and lower lips, and the only thing I could do was let that heal.

The phone let out a rattling ring that was too loud for the small room.

"Mr. Gordon," Julio Moreno greeted me over the line.

"Julio," I responded. "Thanks for getting back to me. Is the line good?"

"Yes," he told me.

"Mine should be," I offered.

"What can I do for you, Chase?" His tone was aloof, as if he was expecting some wild favor.

"Esteban is in serious trouble," I explained.

"You found him?"

"And lost him," I answered. "Juan Moralez has him."

"Has him?" Moreno questioned.

"It seems Moralez is missing some cocaine. He blames Esteban and you."

Moreno huffed. "Did Esteban steal it?"

"No," I told him. "Esteban is loyal to you."

"Why is he out stirring up trouble?"

I sighed. "He is loyal," I repeated. "However, he still has secrets."

"Secrets?" the man questioned.

"He has a daughter," I replied.

"Ah, yes," Moreno stated.

"You know, Julio?"

The Cuban chuckled over the phone. "Esteban never told me, but I would be... What is the word? Remiss. I would be remiss if I wasn't aware of the weaknesses of my men."

"Of course."

"How does Esteban's daughter matter?" Julio asked. "Is Moralez threatening her?"

"She had a boyfriend whose father works for Moralez. This kid stole the cocaine. Something like 250 kilos."

Moreno grunted. "Moralez wants to make a point."

"I think he's already killed the kid," I told him.

"What does Moralez want?" Moreno questioned, as if he expected something more.

"He wants you to replace his missing cocaine."

"That's ridiculous," he admonished.

"And unnecessary," I said. "I don't need it. However, I could use some muscle."

"I can't do that, Chase," he responded with remorse lacing each word.

"C'mon, Julio," I pleaded. "Send the tattooed fellow. What's his name?"

"Jorge," Moreno replied. "I can't help."

"Moralez is going to kill Esteban and Rosalina," I advised.

"It is regrettable," he agreed. "I love Esteban as if he were my son. *Pero...* But, if I do anything, Moralez will use it to start a war. He's a man with no honor. It won't just be my men. He will go after their families. Their wives. Their children."

"You don't need to pony up the coke," I told him. "I found what Victor Berríos stole. It can be used to make the trade."

"That won't matter, Chase," Moreno informed me. "Moralez will kill Esteban, no matter what. The girl, too. He intends to make a point."

He continued, "Juan wants to draw me out. I cannot let him do that. Esteban is working on his own. If Moralez strikes first, I'll deliver a killing blow. But I cannot risk retaliation."

I sighed. "You may condemn them to death. And as it is, Moralez already thinks I work for you. It might be you will receive retaliation no matter what."

"Then I must prepare for that," he acknowledged.

The man breathed heavily into the phone before he added, "Chase, can you help him?" There was a sorrow in his tone. Helplessness too.

"I'm not sure I can do anything without taking Moralez down," I told him. "Where can I find Moralez?"

"Chase," Moreno murmured through the line. "I can't do anything else. I'm sorry."

The line disconnected, leaving me holding the phone. I dropped it back on the receiver. It wasn't something surprising. The conversation played out exactly the way I heard it in my head before I called. Moreno couldn't help. There was more at play between Moralez and Moreno than I knew. I doubted I'd ever get those details, and they didn't matter. Right now, I had to save Rosalina. Somehow, I guessed if I didn't save Rosalina, then it wouldn't help to rescue Scar.

I could charge in and take the two back by force. Moralez had enough men to make that formidable, but the actual issue facing me was I didn't know where to go. The video of Scar looked like it was recorded in a warehouse. Empty warehouses were plentiful in most cities, but somehow ports like Tampa Bay breed those places like cockroaches. They are everywhere, and without so much as a clue, I might as well go back to West Palm Beach, untie *Carina*, and hide out in the Bahamas until this all blew over. It would accomplish the same thing. Honestly, it would at least take me out of harm's way.

My only genuine lead was Berríos. I wondered if Moralez would expect that, too. There were so many factors in play that it would be difficult to know what was being planned.

First, I needed to assume I was under surveillance. Even if I wasn't, to act like I was being followed seemed the safest option. Plan for the worst.

Whatever I did next needed to be soon. While Moreno thought his line wasn't compromised, it was always possible Kohl had it tagged. He could know right where to find me. I needed to move before he sent a couple of uniformed cops to pick me up.

My M45 was under the seat of the rental. I'd carelessly stashed it after I got off the dive boat. At least Gaspar hadn't taken it when he smashed my windows.

I searched for my keys before remembering they were still in the ignition. When Throat Tattoo dragged me out of the car, I didn't have time to pull the keys out.

With my head on a swivel, I marched toward the Versa. At least the windshield remained attached, but there were three spider-webbed cracks spread from three impact spots. It was not only going to be noticeable, but the patterns might make it difficult to see clearly.

Unfortunately, I only had this car.

After brushing all the glass shards off the driver's seat, I slid in and started the engine. I could see well enough to drive. The damage might obstruct some of my peripheral vision, but for the moment, I could move the vehicle.

Being static never worked for me. I spent too many years in hurry-up-and-wait mode. Nothing felt more useless than doing nothing. I realized the value of patience. But when I was angry, frustrated, and aching from a beating, patience barely existed.

Since I needed to move, Berríos made the best target. I drove the car north toward Tampa.

At that time of night, the drive took almost an hour and a half. I stayed on the side streets. The last thing I wanted was a cop to pull me over for the state of my car. Best case, I'd get a ticket. Worst case, my name was already circulating as a person of interest. Any of it would slow me down, and with a deadline of tomorrow, I needed to stay in gear.

The side streets helped me lose anyone following me. I didn't see any lights, but I proceeded with caution.

My mind wandered as I drove. I'd been on land too long now. *Carina* and I needed to vanish after this for a while. This wallowing self-pity I'd immersed myself in the past few months needed to be over.

I knew what the issue was. It was ludicrous, but knowing the ridiculousness of self-loathing doesn't remedy grief. I'd lost too many people recently. Somehow, that was driving me now. I'd be damned if I lost Rosalina and Scar.

After three passes through Berríos's neighborhood, I parked several doors down.

21

The M45 hung casually in my hand, swinging along with my right thigh as I marched across the grass. The neighbors appeared to be all snug on their couches watching whatever drivel came on television.

My gait never slowed as I bee-lined toward the front porch. The yellow bug light illuminated the front step. My right foot planted firmly next to the handle, and the force shattered the wood frame, sending splinters across the living room carpet.

"Aaaa!" Jovina Berríos screamed as the door flew open.

As I came through the door, she grabbed a .38 on the table next to her recliner. The television was droning on—some procedural crime show. The .45 came up in my grip as I charged her.

My left hand balled up and struck her in the face. I don't make it a habit to hit women. There's a sickening sensation I get when I do. Years of Southern, genteel training told me to never hit a girl. However, my CO, Judith Shaw, demanded I give her my best shots if we sparred. She once berated me for holding back, telling me

I was a misogynist for not striking her in the same way I would a man. After that, I didn't hold back–with her.

This blow wasn't a hard one. Just enough to stun her before she fired the .38. Somehow, it seemed better than shooting her.

She grunted with the impact, and I swept the .38 out of her hands before pushing her into the chair.

"What are you doing here?" she cried, tears streaming down her face as she held her nose.

Everything was dramatic. My fist only glanced off her cheek, so the nose was a play. I'm not saying the punch didn't sting, but it wouldn't leave a mark either.

"Sit down," I demanded, shoving the barrel of the M45 toward her.

I stepped back to glance down the hallway. "You alone?" I questioned.

She nodded.

The gun stayed raised as I pushed the door closed. I didn't want any nosy neighbors noticing the busted entryway.

"Where's the hubby?" I asked.

Jovina Berríos stared at me. Her eyes quivered, but I couldn't tell if it was fake or not. This was a woman whose entire life revolved around violent men. She'd learned. Adapted. There were techniques she used to stay under the radar or mitigate the anger.

"Where is your husband?" I asked again, raising the volume of my voice.

She shook her head. Tears welled in already bloodshot eyes. "He's out," she admitted after several seconds.

My head cocked as I stared at her. The woman was filled with emotions.

"Where's Victor?" I asked, thinking I already had the answer. The man Moralez sent to the bar hinted at the truth. Moralez practically confirmed it.

Jovina's head dropped. She knew.

"Did your husband kill him?" I asked. It seemed brutal for a man to murder his own son, even for Juan Moralez. I thought my family was bad, but that seemed incomprehensible.

The woman didn't answer. She inhaled a deep breath and crossed her arms.

"He did, didn't he?" I asked again.

"Are you going to shoot me?"

"That won't help either of us, will it?" I pointed out.

She shifted in her seat, and I explained, "Let me spell that out for you. I don't want to kill you, but I will. Before I do that, though, I'll shoot you in the leg. Maybe the shoulder. If that doesn't stop you, I'll kill you."

Her lungs released the air she'd sucked in. "What do you want?" she asked me.

"You let him kill your son?"

Jovina let her head shift before she stopped the nod.

"You did, didn't you?" I gasped. "Shit, I thought my mother was a bitch. You just made her look like a saint."

The woman sneered at me.

"Why would you do that?"

"Victor made a mistake," she commented. Her tone was icy, but I wasn't sure how authentic it was.

"A mistake?" I repeated. "He was still your son."

"You don't cross a man like Juan Moralez without..."–she paused, as if trying to find the right word–"consequences." Even then, it looked as if she didn't like the choice she made.

"Would he have killed your husband for this?" I questioned.

Jovina shrugged but responded, *"Sí."*

"Where is your husband?" I asked for the third time.

"No sé," she replied. "I don't know."

"Was Victor not worth fighting for?"

She didn't answer.

"Afraid to lose all this." I waved my hand around the room.

"You don't understand," she insisted.

"I understand enough. When will he be back?"

She shrugged.

"Probably grabbing a beer after killing his son, huh?"

Her eyes burned as she tried to bore through me with her pupils.

"You need to deliver a message then," I insisted.

Her head shook. "No, I can't."

Jovina Berríos was a hard woman. It's possible I was being too hard on her. She grew up in a society with little regard for women. They were only useful for fucking, cooking, and raising children. Beyond that, men like Moralez, Moreno, and Berríos had no use for them. Their opinions didn't matter. Nor did their desires or dreams. They were born with one job–marry a man and make him happy.

The culture was prevalent everywhere, even in mainstream America. Women struggled to accomplish half what a man could. It didn't matter how smart either was. Society easily disregards a female genius over a moronic male.

When these thoughts crossed my mind, I thought about the difference between my mother and my former CO. Donna Gordon lived under the thumb of an abusive father and husband. It was her duty because the same preacher that was sleeping with the choir director told her it was the place God wanted her to be. Shaw, on the other hand, grew up under an equally abusive father. However, she learned quickly there was no one to help her. At sixteen, she shot her father in the leg after he broke three ribs. Before he hit the floor, she walked out of the house and never returned.

Now, Shaw was a general. My mother was continuously chasing after my father's affection, and she has dragged my sister down into the muck with her.

I wonder what the difference was.

Without knowing Jovina's history, I guessed it was similar. The timidity about her husband. The acceptance of Victor's murder. She only knew one way to survive, and she would do it.

"I'm not asking," I told her, leaning over her with an intimidating scowl. "I want you to tell your husband. What's his name?"

"Dominico," she whispered.

"Dominico," I repeated, to imprint the name in my mind.

I continued, "I want you to tell Dominico that I'm coming for him."

Her eyes widened. "What do you mean?"

"What I mean," I began, "is I don't care about Moralez. I'll take care of Juan on my own. But Dominico..."

I paused and straightened up. My arms folded with the .45 resting on my left arm. "For Dominico, I plan to make him pay for this."

She trembled but stayed silent.

I added, "Mostly this is for Victor. I'll cut Dominico into little pieces."

Her throat muscles spasmed as she swallowed hard.

For added measure, I smiled. "Whatever he did to Victor will seem like nothing compared to what I do."

"He won't let you," she finally whimpered.

"Is there anything about me that looks like I need his permission?" I hissed, sending spittle toward her.

For a split second, her countenance betrayed her. Was it relief? Joy? It was so minute, and had I not been staring into her face, I might have missed it. She only needed a split second to regain her composure–to become the obedient concubine. But in that moment, she revealed it would thrill her to see him dead.

"You'd like that, wouldn't you?" I asked, letting my voice show a glimmer of glee.

She didn't answer. Her stoic wife routine was firmly in place.

"Don't worry," I promised. "I'll let him know it was you that asked for it."

"No!" she gasped.

I offered a maniacal grin, attempting to impress fear upon her. I wanted her to worry that I would tell him it was her. She'd been with the man for decades, and my promise to come after him seemed empty. He'd survived more than me. Jovina expected him to survive this, too. That scared her. Enough that she'd deliver my message, if for no other reason than to denounce my threat to expose her as Dominico's betrayer.

"Don't move," I ordered as I backed into the kitchen. She remained in my sight, and the .45 stayed in hers.

I found what I wanted–a roll of plastic wrap in a drawer next to the stove.

Plastic wrap works extremely effectively for binding someone. It was a trick I learned in high school. In rural Arkansas, the only place to party was an empty field. Someone brought a keg, dropped it in a cooler of ice, and poured beer all night long. The first person to pass out ended up stripped of his clothes and wrapped to a tree, usually one closest to the road. Eight or nine layers of plastic wrap were unbreakable.

I wrapped Jovina around her torso, pushing her arms down to the side. After she was tightly secured, I bound her feet to the chair. My plan would work better if a few hours passed. Given the chance, Jovina would call her husband seconds after I left the house. This way, he'd have the shock of seeing her when he came through the door.

"Make sure you tell your husband 'goodbye,'" I teased her sadistically. "It will be the last time you see him."

The act left me dirty, but I lost any sympathy for a woman who wouldn't protect her own child. It didn't matter the reason, she let Dominico kill Victor. If my actions left me soiled but Rosalina safe, it was worth it.

Without a look back, I turned off the lights and pulled the door closed. As usual, the Florida air was sticky. I walked toward the street and vanished into the shadows, waiting for my trap to be sprung.

22

It took Dominico Berríos five hours to come home–almost one in the morning. I sat across the street in a copse of bushes, watching the house. The gangster pulled up in the same black Lincoln that he dragged me off in a few days ago. This time, he was alone. It was the end of his day, and he didn't have his same entourage. I wondered for a second if Goon's body floated back to shore yet.

As soon as the lights in the house came on, I heard the reaction, even from across the street. The front door wouldn't latch after I broke the doorjamb, and the sound of crying and shouting emanated from inside. After several seconds, the crying turned to screaming, mostly in Spanish. A crash echoed from the open door, and Dominico Berríos stormed out of the house, marching toward the black Lincoln.

Jovina appeared in the lighted doorway, leaning against the door frame. Her face was bloody, and her right hand held the left forearm gingerly. Berríos may have broken her arm. I seethed inside, a little at myself for leaving her in that position. Mostly, I aimed the rage at Berríos. By the time the night was done, I'd make him pay for hitting his wife. He was going to suffer for killing Victor. I wanted to see him tremble when he faced me.

The driver's door slammed on the Lincoln, and he backed out of the driveway. I bounced to my feet and sprinted toward the shattered Versa parked around the corner. Before he made it out of the neighborhood, I was trailing behind him with my lights off.

Berríos drove like a NASCAR driver until he reached the interstate. Once we reached a busier road, I cut my lights on and stayed six car lengths behind him.

The thug pulled onto I-75, heading south. As he shot down the interstate, he sped up to ninety miles per hour. I didn't think he was trying to lose me or even noticed I was following him. No; he was in a hurry to get to his location.

Since I first talked to Moreno, I struggled with why I was helping Scar. I considered us diametric opposites. We stood for different things.

At first, it was just for the adrenaline rush. Something to mask the grief I had been wallowing in. Since Jorge and his partner approached me in Pat's, thoughts of Allie waned. They weren't gone, but I'd slid them into a corner.

Now, my bets were on the table. Scar was doing something I understood. Driven to protect his daughter, he would die for her. It didn't seem to matter he never shared a word with her. For him, it was the moral thing to do. I not only respected that, but I also felt compelled to help him now.

Plus, something about the thug was irritatingly likable.

We drove south for almost two hours, which in Florida street time didn't equate to a great distance. I tried to stay focused on the Lincoln's taillights, and I stopped paying attention to the signs on the side of the road. Until the light on my gas gauge dinged, I wasn't worried about how far he planned to drive. I'd even gotten used to the road noise and wind created from four missing windows. The Versa's dash alerted me to how many miles I had until I was empty. The countdown started as soon as the little yellow light next to the gas symbol came on. It read thirty-five miles.

There wasn't much to do, but hope Berríos was nearing his destination.

As if on command, the Lincoln pulled off onto the Tamiami Trail. The exit sign stated it was the Englewood exit. I stayed a few cars behind him as he merged onto the Trail, heading northwest.

He slowed as he moved along the streets. He turned north on Highway 776. After a mile, he turned left onto a residential street. I took a chance and killed my lights before following him onto the road. I pulled over to the right curb and crept along, hoping to appear like nothing more than a parked car.

The red dots from the Lincoln's taillights turned left, and I pulled off the side of the road to race down the street. When I made the turn, I found myself on a dead-end street that stretched half a mile toward Lemon Bay, the stretch of water between the mainland and the barrier islands on the west.

I stopped at the curb again. My headlights were still off, but I could see clearly from the LED streetlights illuminating the road. Eight houses lined each side of the street all the way to the end. The lots didn't appear large, but the houses were all sizable–at least four thousand square feet each. The developer built the neighborhood on a small jut into the bay. Each side of the peninsula had deep-water slips and boat houses.

The Lincoln sat in the fifth driveway on the right with its headlights still lighted up, allowing Berríos a few seconds to see his way to the door.

With the streetlights beaming so brightly, my shattered windows and busted windshield would stand out on this street. For now, the edge of the street where I parked was just outside of the lights, leaving my car obscured in the shadows.

My head turned to study the seawall on the back side of the finger of land. From where I was sitting, I noticed the patios between the houses and the canal didn't have as much light. The homeowners might want to sit on the patio and pretend to watch the stars. Too much light would drown it out.

I climbed out of the Versa and slunk around the trunk. My feet padded across the lawn closest to me. It was almost three in the morning–most of the residents were sleeping. The few not nestled in their beds shouldn't be staring out their windows. Still, it was always best to stay low and move fast. Too often people think if they creep slowly, they'll be less likely to be seen. It just doesn't work that way. The slower you are, the longer the human eye has to register what it is seeing. If one was perfectly still, he might be invisible in the right situation, but he won't get anywhere. It's always better to create a lower profile and cover the ground swiftly. In those cases, someone might catch movement, but by the time the eyes take a second look, the subject should be in a different place altogether.

It was never foolproof. All plans were subject to Murphy's Law. So far, though, it hadn't steered me wrong.

I reached the seawall with no spotlights tagging me. No alarms sounded.

The stench of stale sea water drifted up. The canal was only a few hundred feet wide, and with no outlet, the trash from the bay floated down the canal but never came out. I didn't need to see the surface of the water to know it was full of floating beer cans, chunks of Styrofoam, rotting seaweed, and at least a handful of dead fish. No one wanted to swim in this water. If anything, it should make the owners of these homes consider how much they spend on the location simply to become the garbage chute for Lemon Bay.

As I tightroped my way down the wall, I noticed the backyards of all these houses were virtually without grass. Any shrubbery or plants were in pots scattered around a concrete patio. If an owner opted for the grass, it seemed to be a six-inch strip along the seawall. Something the yard guy might spend three minutes with an electric weed whacker once a week to keep trimmed.

As I neared the edge of the fifth yard, I noticed the lights on inside the house. I tried to will myself as far to the edge of the seawall as possible, hoping to stay out of sight.

At the edge of the canal, a covered dock jutted over the seawall where a sixty-foot Hatteras yacht floated next to the pier. If I reached the covered pier, there would be a straight-shot view into the house while I remained in the shadows of the ten-inch posts supporting the structure.

Three figures were moving inside. I recognized Berríos and Moralez as they passed in front of the open window. Berríos seemed agitated as he talked, moving his hands in wild, sweeping motions. The third man was much younger. I guessed around my age, give or take a few years. I didn't have a decent enough view of him to distinguish his features, but I didn't think I'd encountered him before.

The younger one kept making motions as if he was trying to urge Berríos to quiet down. Dominico ignored him. His face grew redder as he talked, and while I couldn't hear him, the expressions he made indicated he was almost shouting. The creaking of the boats and squealing of the dock lines rubbing against the wooden piers echoed through the canal, drowning out anything the men inside said. Moralez continued to shake his head while the younger man tried to calm Berríos. Finally, Moralez lifted his hand, his face glazed with a stern glare. He took command of the room and pointed toward the double doors, directing the other two men out of the house. Berríos nodded and walked toward the doors leading out to the patio.

I inhaled sharply. If they came outside, the three of them would almost certainly spot me. It would take me a hair over two seconds to pull the .45 and shoot all three of them. Would that seal Scar and Rosalina's fate?

As Moralez reached for the door, I glanced over my shoulder at the canal and considered my options.

23

As the three men moved toward the exit, I turned and climbed aboard the Hatteras. My hands and feet scaled around to the opposite side, where I could hang on to the port side of the flybridge without being seen by the three men.

"Calm down, Dom," Moralez insisted as they crossed the concrete patio. "There isn't anything to worry about."

"The fuck there isn't," Berríos stated. "The bastard was in my house. He practically raped my wife."

I sighed at the accusation. Was Berríos just trying to exaggerate? To ensure Moralez took action?

"By this time tomorrow, he'll be dead," the younger man promised.

Peering around the flybridge, I had a better view of the third man. He was in his late twenties, and his facial features resembled Moralez. His son, maybe.

"The man killed Miguel," Berríos told them. "He must have swum back."

Miguel must have been the Goon I dragged under with me.

"No one is unkillable," the young Moralez snapped as he ushered Berríos onto the back of the Hatteras. His accent was minimal–the type a second-generation kid picked up in his home and community. Moralez probably sent this kid to college to get a business degree in order to run the drug smuggling business efficiently.

Berríos grunted a half-hearted agreement. "He came into my house," he repeated. "Twice."

"Do you want me to send someone over there?" Moralez offered as he opened the sliding door on the aft deck. "In case he comes back."

The son asked, "Did Gordon say anything about my father?"

Good call, Chase. I knew it was his son.

The younger man closed the glass doors as Berríos answered, "He told Jovina he didn't care about you, sir. Just that he was coming after me."

One of the Moralez men turned on the lights in the salon, and rays of light shot through the windows. I crept down the side of the boat until I could peek through the porthole. Don't get too close, I reminded myself. As long as I kept my face a foot away from the glass, the men inside shouldn't be able to see me. Unless they turned out the interior lights.

One thing about boats, especially ones kept in warm climates, is often the owners have a vent or fan cycling air through the cabin. It helps prevent mildew–an ongoing battle for almost every boat owner. Generally, the sound inside will slip out of those openings. While I had to strain to hear their words as the early morning breeze drifted along the canal from the bay, I heard what they said.

"Why isn't he worried about me?" Moralez questioned. It was justified, confusing, and exactly what I wanted.

"He doesn't think he can get near you," his son commented.

Moralez snarled in disbelief.

"What are we going to do about it?" Berríos demanded in a tone he realized too late was harsher than either Moralez normally allowed.

"In the morning," Moralez explained, "we'll call in our debt. I doubt Julio Moreno is going to put up anything to save his man, but I'll deal with him in due time. We kill the girl and Velasquez. Then, we focus everything on finding Gordon."

"Won't be hard," the son quipped. "We've tracked him twice now."

"I had our man in the Tampa PD look into him," young Moralez continued. "He was Special Forces in the Marines."

I rolled my eyes. Recon would roll over the Army Special Forces like it was a limp kitten. Most of the Special Forces guys I knew would disagree, but I trusted my gut with it. That this kid didn't know the difference irritated me more than it should have. It wasn't like I didn't have a plethora of reasons to hate him. This one seemed petty.

"He's going to come after me if you don't find him first," Berríos pleaded.

"Don't worry, Dom," Moralez encouraged him. "He won't find you. We're going to hide you until this blows over."

"Right," the son confirmed. "We can stash you somewhere until we find him. Eventually he'll go back to his bar in West Palm."

"I want to kill him," Berríos asserted. "Bastard should be mine."

"Don't worry, my friend. He will pay for all the trouble he's put us through. Especially what he's done to you."

"I want to make him suffer," the man attested.

"Dom, you've done enough," Moralez assured him. "You handled Victor for me."

"I'm sorry about that, sir," Berríos offered.

"I know," the older man replied. "It's tough when our children disappoint us. But you did your part to fix it."

"I should have found the shipment," he told the drug lord.

"Yes, but it's done now. You did the job."

"How about a drink?" the kid suggested.

"It's late," Berríos pointed out.

"Or early," Moralez joked. "Why don't we have a quick one, Dom? After that, you can stay here until tomorrow."

"Jovina?" the man asked.

"I'll send Gaspar over to get her in the morning," Moralez promised. "Gordon's looking for you. I think Jovina will be safe until then."

"Armado," Moralez addressed his son. "Make us three drinks. Rum, Dom?"

Berríos nodded, relaxing some.

Armado Moralez walked to a small bar built into the salon's bulkhead. He lifted a round bottle of brown liquor. I couldn't identify the label, but it didn't matter, just a split second of occupational curiosity. He pulled two glasses down from a rack and poured a couple of inches into each one. As he reached up for a third glass, the younger Moralez paused. Instead, he turned as if to ask a question. His hand came up with a small .22 Smith & Wesson pistol.

The report sounded like someone smashing a full bottle of soda—a soft popping sound. Berríos didn't flinch or jerk when the .22 bullet hit his face. He slumped to the floor like someone released the air from him. He almost looked like a dog coiled on the floor for a nap.

Armado set the Smith & Wesson on the bar before handing Juan Moralez the glass of rum. The elder saluted his son with the tumbler in his hand.

"Didn't get any on the carpet," Moralez mused, as if his son had scored a goal.

Armado sipped the rum with a smug smile. "He was going to be a problem," the younger Moralez commented.

"Should we have Gaspar pick up Jovina?" the senior asked.

Armado shrugged.

"Take the boat out," Moralez told his son. "Get rid of him. We'll deal with Velasquez in the morning."

"I could wait and make one trip," he suggested to his father.

Juan Moralez shook his head. "I don't want to shuffle bodies through my house," he admonished. "I'll have Gaspar and Orlando take care of Velasquez and the girl."

"Will Moreno get his hands dirty?" Armado asked.

"No," Moralez admitted. "He's not stupid. Julio will keep his head down for now."

"We need to drive up to his little restaurant and shoot him," Armado insisted.

Moralez shook his head in disbelief. "Do you think the Feds aren't watching him there? The man is like clockwork, and some agent would get pictures of us."

"What will we do?" the son asked.

"No, Moreno will lose his second tomorrow. He'll replace him, but Velasquez was a force to be reckoned with. Now, he'll open up. Our chance will come soon."

As I listened to Moralez discuss making a move on Moreno, I wondered if the entire affair was a feint to draw Moreno out. It didn't seem likely. How could so many things be twisted to line up? I doubted it, but time had taught me anything was possible. My gut told me Moralez saw an opportunity. Perhaps he realized the connection between Rosalina and Scar, or he just took advantage when Scar showed up on his radar. Whatever the thought process, Moralez was drooling over Moreno's piece of pie. No matter what Moreno did, war was going to break out. From the sound of it, Moralez played a long game. Kill Scar and wait for Julio to grow comfortable with a new protector—someone far inferior to Scar. Moralez was counting on Moreno dropping his guard. I wasn't sure Moreno's guard ever fell.

"I'm going back to bed," Moralez announced. He pointed at Berríos's crumpled form, ordering Armado, "Get rid of him."

"Yes, Papa," the man agreed.

Moralez swallowed the rum in his glass and handed the tumbler back to Armado as if he was a waiter. He offered his child a curt nod before he left. I watched Juan Moralez return to the house.

Armado moved to the helm in the pilothouse. The large diesels rumbled to life, sputtering exhaust for the first few seconds before the sound evened out. I slid down to the starboard deck, trying to cower to the side as Armado emerged onto the port side. He began untying the dock lines, beginning at the bow. Other than sliding in the filmy water, my only option was to stay hidden until he got away from land.

I heard the revolutions of the engine go up as Armado throttled the two diesel engines. The vessel inched off the dock. Once it was off the pier, Armado executed a 180-degree turn, spinning the bow of the boat around to face the bay. The hull shook as the motors pushed the sixty-foot yacht out of the canal at idle speed.

From the pilothouse, Armado couldn't see me. As long as he stayed there, the canted forward windows limited his view to the bow. He'd have to turn to look aft, and I expected he might do that a few times as he maneuvered the boat into the bay.

There wasn't much traffic on the water at this time of night, but within an hour, the bay would light up with fishing boats zipping out before dawn to get their catch.

The air was chilly at this time of night. I wished for a sweatshirt, but it wouldn't be anything I couldn't survive. I let my head lean back on the deck as we motored south through the bay. The more distance we put between us and the shoreline, the brighter the stars grew. Fields of white dots scattered across the clear sky.

My arm looped through the life line so my hand could reach the stanchion. I wasn't watching forward, and one enormous wave could flop me into the sea if I didn't see it coming.

A plan unfolded in my head. Like Moralez's strategy for taking down Moreno, this one was borne of circumstance. Juan and Armado Moralez opened up an opportunity. I just needed to play the hand.

My head lolled to starboard, and I watched the outline of the barrier islands. The lights dotting along the strip of land grew scarcer as we neared the southern tip. Once we passed the last gleaming orb of civilization, I studied the shapes of rocky shore dipping beneath the surface. Beyond it was the black of the unlit ocean. A few random dots pinpointed the smattering of boats afloat at this time of night.

Once the Hatteras moved out of the bay, the bow veered south. The only light out here glowed from the cabin's ports. After another glance, I confirmed we were alone out here. The closest light was over a mile to starboard.

Armado followed the coastline, but he maintained about a mile distance between the boat and shore. If I were him, I'd worry about a Coast Guard Cutter or even the local Marine Police showing up for an inspection. He might have a hard time explaining the dead body in the salon.

We were far enough out, and I needed to implement my plan before he reached his destination. I rolled over to my hands and knees and crawled aft.

24

I slipped the M45 out of the waistband of my shorts as I climbed gingerly down to the aft deck. The sliding doors were closed. If Armado glanced back, the interior lights reflecting back should mask me. But I needed to get inside–without alarming him. Even if the doors opened without a sound, the engine noise, coupled with the waves and wind, created a din that Armado would immediately notice.

If I waited until the next wave jolted the boat into a roll, I could slide the door open a bit. Armado might mistake it for opening as the waves rocked the yacht. With luck, he might look back and ignore it once the initial alarm passed.

I could see the helm. Armado stood, stationed at the wheel just forward of the salon. The lights in the pilothouse were off, allowing him to see forward. But he left the salon lighted.

The .22 pistol remained on the bar where Armado left it, shifting from side to side with each wave. There was no guarantee he didn't have another weapon on him. The little Smith & Wesson was convenient and quieter than larger calibers. Perfect for murdering someone without the neighbors noticing.

If Armado carried another gun, he'd have plenty of time to shoot at me before I crossed the salon. I didn't want him dead. There was a better use for him, and it required his breathing.

The younger Moralez leaned over the helm, studying the chart plotter. With a few swipes of his fingers, he adjusted the heading a few degrees, veering the vessel southwest a bit more. The engines slowed. He was moving toward some deeper water. As long as he made it out there without drawing any attention, he could drop to idle, tie an anchor to Berríos, and drop him in about sixty feet of water.

The hull rocked as he shifted directions. By the time I felt the side-to-side motion, I missed my opportunity to slide the door open.

Armado moved away from the helm, and I stepped aft toward the stern. He set the auto-pilot before descending some steps. As soon as he was out of sight, I started forward. The sliding door swooshed, and I slipped inside, shutting it quickly. Two seconds. I hoped during that time he wasn't able to hear down below. The motors should be loudest down below, drowning out most of the sounds up here.

I stepped over Berríos, moving across the salon. Sticky brown blood discolored the rug.

The galley was roomy and situated on the port side. There wasn't a direct line of sight from the helm to it, and I pressed myself against the stove, waiting with my .45 raised.

Armado shuffled up the steps, and the chart plotter beeped as he adjusted the heading again. The yacht turned back toward shore several degrees as he pulled back on the throttles. The engines slowed to idle.

I leaned forward to see him checking the radar–in case any fishing boats were hiding in the dark. Satisfied, he walked past the galley, stepping over Berríos and out onto the aft deck. He never noticed me when he walked through the cabin. Careless. He expected to be alone, and his brain wasn't searching for trouble on board.

My knees bent, and I lowered myself behind the counter. As I cowered on the galley floor, I wondered how far Moralez planned to play this game. Berríos obviously ran his course with the man. Was he worried that sending him after his own son broke him? Or was it just that I targeted him?

Now I realized Jovina might be in danger, too. She might not have the details–I suspect Berríos didn't talk too much about work. But she knew enough to realize who was ultimately responsible for her son's death. At least with Berríos alive, he might contain her. Now, she'd be a loose cannon waiting to fire. Moralez couldn't afford to let her live. In fact, if I didn't pull everything off in the next few hours, Scar and Rosalina stood a slight chance of surviving the day. At least, the way he spoke to Armado sounded like they were going to be among the breathing for a little while. But he also didn't expect me to bring the coke, so his imposed deadline may be arbitrary. Once his patience ran out, he might kill them without waiting for me.

My head stretched to peek over the counter. Now, I had the same problem Armado would have experienced. The

LED salon lights reflected everything in the doors. The glass might as well be a mirror. However, I had a slight advantage over him. I knew someone was out there. If I stared long enough, I could make out a foot and a calf on the deck. It took a few seconds for my brain to realize Armado was kneeling over the storage locker, looking for something.

I twisted around and pulled open a couple of drawers. The third drawer below the microwave had the plastic wrap. If it worked for Jovina, I thought it might do the same with Armado. It would help if I found some zip ties or line to secure him first, but at least I had something. I dropped back down and waited.

It didn't take too long. The door swooshed open, and Armado grunted as he came inside. I stood, raising the M45 level with him. He froze in the doorway. A thirty-pound plow anchor rested on his left shoulder.

"Who the fuck are you?" he cursed, glancing at the .22 on the bar.

"Let's not try for it," I suggested. "I'd have to gun you down before you took a step."

"Gordon?" he questioned.

I offered him a smile. "Where'd you go to college?" I asked.

Armado stared at me, dumbfounded.

"No, seriously." I repeated the question. "Where did you go to college?"

"Florida State," he responded.

"What was your major?" I asked.

"Why the fuck do you want to know that?" he demanded.

"Because I'm holding the gun," I pointed out. "Mostly, I'm curious if I was correct."

"Correct?" he stammered.

I shrugged, twisting the gun sideways for a split second. It was a pointless move, but everyone's seen it on television. It's supposed to be intimidating. Personally, I thought I should intimidate him enough without the theatrics, but I wasn't sure he didn't lack the brains needed to obey me.

He continued to glare at me.

"Major?" I questioned again.

"Business," he finally answered. "Why?"

"Like I said, I wanted to know if I was right."

"What do you think you're going to do here?" he asked boldly. "Kill me?"

"Not if you don't make me," I told him. "Turn around."

He shifted his weight to pull the anchor off his shoulder.

"Don't do that," I ordered. "In fact, put your free hand against the glass door."

He groaned when he did as I demanded. The barrel of the .45 remained aimed at him while I walked up behind him. I gave him a quick pat down. He didn't have a weapon, but I took his wallet and phone.

"Okay, gently put that anchor down," I said.

His shoulder shrugged the weight off it, letting his hand lower it to the sole.

"Planning to dump poor Dominico?" I asked.

He didn't answer.

"Back up and sit in that chair," I told him, pointing my head toward a folding director's chair.

"My father won't put up with this," he growled.

I shrugged. "We shall see," I stated. "I'd worry right now about what I'll put up with."

"You don't look that tough," he snarled at me.

I ignored his taunt as I pulled the plastic wrap off the counter.

"What the hell are you doing with that?" he demanded. His voice trembled as he exclaimed, "You said you would not kill me!"

"Shut up," I snapped. "I told you I wouldn't if you didn't force me. Talking too much annoys me, and I know a permanent way to stop that."

Armado glanced down. The murderer who gunned down Dominico Berríos a couple of hours ago vanished, replaced by a boy who wanted to prove himself a man. I took advantage of his silence and wound the plastic around his torso. He surprised me by not struggling. It wasn't fear. I mean, there was a little fear. Mostly, he thought this was an annoyance. Perhaps Daddy would show up to bail him out.

Once I assured myself he couldn't move, I tossed the plastic wrap on the counter. We were still drifting, and like Armado, I wanted to get out of here before someone came to investigate.

The sliding door leading to the aft deck hung open. As I stepped around Armado, I flung his cellphone into the water before closing the door. He grimaced at me—some attempt to appear menacing. I hated to tell him that even when he wasn't bound to a chair, there was nothing threatening about him. He hadn't learned that from Daddy yet.

I climbed the steps into the pilothouse. The chart plotter indicated we were fifteen miles off Cayo Costa State Park in roughly thirty-five feet of water. We were a little south of Boca Grande, which worked out better for me. I typed the coordinates into the chart plotter and marked the heading. The engines roared as I throttled them down. I didn't want to go too slow. Time was running out.

The hull planed out at seventeen knots, and I spun around to study Armado.

"You got any dive gear?" I questioned him.

"Why?" he asked.

"Dammit, you don't learn," I explained, waving the pistol at him. "I don't need a reason."

"It's next to the engine room," he finally admitted.

"See," I encouraged him. "The more you work with me, the better it is for you."

He glanced down at the layers of plastic binding him to the chair, as if wondering how his situation was better than anything else.

"I could stack you on top of Dominico like cord wood," I pointed out.

His eyes shifted to the corpse.

"Is his wife in danger?" I asked.

"Whose?" he questioned me. I wondered if this was what having children felt like—a constant argument with oneself about why one shouldn't shoot them.

"Berríos."

"No," he answered.

I folded my arms and stared at him.

"No," he reiterated. "Not yet, at least."

"When this is said and done, I want her left alone," I urged.

He nodded quickly.

"How did you get aboard?" he asked after a few minutes.

"I'm stealthy," I quipped in explanation. "You'll never know if I'm around."

He stared at me with skepticism.

"Where are Velasquez and the girl?"

Armado shook his head. "I'm not telling you," he insisted.

I lifted the gun again to show him.

"If I tell you, you'll kill me."

I groaned. It didn't matter, but I wanted to shoot him. The helm stool spun around, and I faced the chart plotter again. At this speed, we'd reach the coordinates in less than twenty minutes.

Eventually, I needed to leave Armado alone. The binding was secure enough. I trusted the younger Moralez couldn't get free. I checked the autopilot one more time before I went below.

He didn't lie. The closet next to the engine room had two BCD, four cylinders, and several snorkel sets, complete with fins. I dragged out enough gear to get me down. When I carried it up the steps, I found Armado hadn't moved. He continued to carry a smug air about him, as if he was positive this situation would remedy itself.

After hooking the BCD and regulator to the cylinder, I returned down below to get the second BCD. Hooked on the wall, I found a submersible flashlight with a snap hook to attach to the front of a BCD. I grabbed it as well. As I passed through the galley, I rifled through the cabinets until I found a roll of trash bags. These were the good ones–designed for bagging leaves with a thicker exterior. Perfect.

The alarm sounded on the helm, and I climbed onto the stool, pulling the throttle back.

"What are you doing?" he asked.

The anchor windlass switch on the helm lowered the anchor until twenty-five feet of chain rattled out of the locker.

"I'm about to take a short swim," I explained.

He stared at me before lifting an eyebrow. The realization struck him, and he blurted out, "You know where the coke is?"

I gave him a nod as I walked behind his chair. My hands pushed down on the back, tilting Armado and chair onto its back legs.

"What the hell?" he shouted as I dragged him down the steps to the head.

I shoved the chair, Armado and all, into the head. After checking that the plastic hadn't loosened during transit, I closed the door to the bathroom. I found a coil of rope in the closet with the scuba gear. The end of the line wound through the latch, and I tied it so Armado couldn't get it open from the inside. If he was free of the chair, he had the strength to break the door. I hoped he was secure enough for the time being.

The night sky was gray now as the sun was coming up on the other side of the state. I was right over the cocaine I'd moved yesterday. Or at least within a hundred feet of it.

I was lucky this time to find a weight belt, but my luck ran out when the only wetsuit down below was a small. My leg wouldn't fit into it.

There was no choice. I'd have to brave the cold for a few minutes. It wasn't the worst I'd ever endured, but I gritted my teeth as I dropped into the water.

25

With the deflated BCD under my right arm, I released the air from the BCD I was wearing. Bubbles raced to the surface as my body sank. The sun had yet to rise, so my visibility remained limited. The gray-purple of the sky turned dark. My hand fumbled around the front of my BCD until it pressed the button on the light hanging off my chest. A diffused beam stretched downward, dancing through the abyss as I descended.

The seafloor was only twenty-five feet deep, and when I settled into the sand, I glanced up. The morning light wasn't breaking through the depths yet. Once dawn broke, the blue sky would illuminate the bottom. For now, all I could see was a grayish tint above me. As I rested on the bottom, I unclipped the flashlight and strafed it across the sand until I located the curved metal of the Hatteras's anchor.

Like I did yesterday, I wanted to use it as my landmark, performing a search radius from the plow anchor. The cooler filled with Moralez's cocaine was close. I knew the coordinates where I dropped the box were exact, but the Hatteras had enough time to swing around the anchor. Once the sun came up, I should even be able to see the rectangular white box. After the anchor set, I considered waiting an hour to give the sun time to rise so I could see on the seafloor. But like I already mentioned, waiting wasn't always a strong suit of mine. In order to save Scar, I didn't have the luxury to wait. Every second longer I took gave old Murphy a chance to enact his law.

My first foray took me north approximately a hundred feet, give or take a body's length. When I came to a stop, I found only an empty seafloor in the beam of light. I shifted my heading southwest, attempting to circle the anchor. I pedaled my feet, pushing myself through the cold water. Several fish darted toward my light, curious to see what was intruding into their world. Most were only small ones I couldn't identify, feeding off the particles settling to the bottom. Twice, a blue crab scampered out of the beam, startled by my sudden approach.

When my calculations told me I'd made a quarter of the way around the edge of my search circle, I paused, floating a foot above the bottom. The compass showed my heading to be on course, and I flashed the beam east. The end of the light didn't reach the anchor. If I was still a hundred feet away, the light wasn't strong enough to spotlight it from here. I had to trust my navigational skills, something I had no trouble doing. As long as one knew how to read a compass, staying on course wasn't always hard. At least in such a small area. At sea, I would still need a few guide signs. Stars usually worked for that, but I didn't trust my celestial skills yet. Although it had been on my bucket list and while I practiced a few times, it wasn't a skill I'd mastered yet. I was not ready to abandon the electronic era. Without my chart plotter, I'd miss more than one island simply by misjudging by a few degrees.

The ocean floor took shape as the sun must have climbed over the horizon. Ripples of sand appeared, but my sight line remained limited as the night sky clung to the west.

I adjusted my heading and kicked my fins, swimming southeast in an arc. Another crab scurried out of my way. He was a big one, measuring almost seven inches across. My eyes followed the little behemoth running in fear. I pulled my toes up to stop my forward motion. A square outline sat roughly fifty feet south of me. I turned and swam toward it.

The white cooler settled at an angle in the sand. One side pointed toward the surface.

My knee pulled up as I came to rest them on the sandy bottom. With the ever-increasing light, I didn't need the flashlight to see the latches on the box. The snap hook clipped easily to my BCD, where I let it hang. The beam of light still shot out from it as it dangled.

I unfolded the plastic bag where I'd stashed it in the pocket of the BCD. My right knee held the deflated vest I'd been carrying. After seeing how tightly the bricks of cocaine had been wrapped, I wasn't concerned with the powder in the water. The plastic should be watertight, and if it wasn't, I didn't need to worry. There would be very little escaping into the water, and frankly, I didn't care if the salt water ruined the drugs or not. As long as I could deliver them.

I began transferring the bricks from the cooler into the plastic bag. I didn't want the hassle of handling the cooler again. Plus, the Hatteras didn't have a dingy davit. Instead, the tender lay mounted on the forward deck. Without a decent winch, I'd need to either haul the weighted box up by hand or rig it off the anchor windlass. One seemed too much work, while the other might take too long.

The plastic bag wasn't perfect. Not only was I filling it with about 250 kilograms of tightly packed bricks of cocaine, seawater flowed in as soon as I opened it up. It would weigh over 250 kilograms.

It took several minutes to fill the bag. Once every brick was in it, I attempted to close it, pulling the sides tight against the bricks. Once I felt I'd wrapped as tightly as I could under the water, I used the belt on the deflated BCD to bind it inside the vest.

BCDs connect to the regulator with a quick-connection that snaps into the inflator. I removed the hose connecting the air supply to the BCD I was wearing, attaching it to the other one. As soon as I connected the hose, I pressed the button to inflate it. The swooshing of air filling the vest's bladder seemed to echo underwater.

The vest inflated, lifting the cocaine and me off the bottom. I wrapped my legs and arm around the ascending package as I pulled the hose free. With my weight and the weight of the cocaine, my ascent was slow, and I kicked my fins to push me up. When I popped through the surface, I steadied the other BCD while I attached the hose to mine.

Within a few seconds, the vest I wore inflated, easing my struggle to stay on the surface.

The Hatteras floated two hundred feet from me, and I rolled to my back and kicked my fins. The BCD and bag of coke dragged behind me as I swam back to the boat. After about fifty feet, I felt the bag shift inside the BCD. Before it came loose and sank back to the bottom, I checked to make sure the cocaine was secure before proceeding to the boat.

The sun had fully risen by the time I came up. Across the water, I heard the screaming of an outboard somewhere in the distance. It could have been anywhere and was probably a fisherman heading out to drop a hook.

Once I dragged the bag onto the swim platform, I sighed with relief. The fear that my makeshift barge wouldn't support the weighted bag or the package might slide off while I swam worried me every inch back. Now, I heaved it from the swim platform, letting seawater pour from it until the burden lightened by at least a hundred pounds. The black garbage bag spilled onto the aft deck as I rolled it over the railing.

After shedding my gear, I found Armado still tightly bound in the head.

"What are you doing?" he insisted. "You need to let me out of here."

I ignored his outburst and slammed the door, leaving him in the head.

"I need to pee," he begged.

"You're in the bathroom," I told him. "Just do it."

"Ugh," he groaned. "That's disgusting."

While he continued to shout protests, I flipped the switch to raise the anchor. The chain clunked into the anchor locker, echoing through the hull. I leaned over to study the charts, searching for a good anchorage. It needed to be some place far enough from civilization to be unnoticed, but close enough to reach a decent dock.

I found two viable locations. Both were about seventy miles south of the Hatteras's current location. At full speed, I could get there in three hours.

A roar came from the engines as I pressed the throttles down. We were between twenty-eight and thirty knots according to the SOG meter, which measures "Speed Over Ground." I set the waypoint in the chart plotter and activated the auto-pilot. I was close enough to shore that it would be important to keep a close watch. However, I ensured the water ahead was clear of any boats, and I stepped into the galley, where I found a box of Pop-Tarts. Cinnamon and brown sugar. When I got back to the helm, I settled in with the cold breakfast pastry and watched the water ahead.

My timing was off, and the trip took almost four hours. The yacht's speed slowed as the surface conditions grew choppy. I found the first anchorage three hours and forty-three minutes after leaving. The inlet was perfect—just southwest of Everglades City. Mangroves covered the shoreline. The depth gauge showed twelve feet as I motored slowly inland. As I studied the growth, I decided swimming here might not be advisable. While I didn't see the eyes sticking up in the brackish waters,

I guessed more than a couple of gators were lurking just under the surface.

Armado continued shouting at me. He'd break for a few minutes before starting back up.

As I lowered the anchor, I considered allowing him to get a bathroom break, but the idea passed. It wasted time. Instead, I checked his bindings. For safe measure, I added another layer. The man was sweating profusely. I brought him a water bottle and poured it in his mouth.

"You have to let me out," he pleaded. His threats waned a couple of hours ago, replaced by begging mixed with some crying.

"Later," I told him.

"Gordon, please," he cried as I closed the door again.

As I glanced at the body on the floor, I was glad I was getting off the boat soon. Berríos had been dead almost six hours, and even if the air conditioner cooled the boat, the Florida heat and humidity would do quite a job on a corpse. By the end of the day, the smell would be atrocious.

After taking several minutes, I moved every brick of cocaine into a locker in the salon. I wiped the .22 down and unloaded it.

"What are you doing?" Armado asked as I put the empty gun in his lap.

"Just leaving you a gift," I told him as I retied the rope, securing the door.

"Come back," he insisted.

I spent fifteen minutes wiping any prints I left from the dive gear, helm, and doors before lowering the eight-foot tender into the water. I twisted the throttle when the two-horse-power motor mounted on the stern puttered to life.

Based on the charts, there should be a dock about eighteen miles north on Marco Island. The little outboard only pushed the boat about eight knots, and the choppy water drenched me as I bashed north until I could navigate through the Ten Thousand Islands, a chain of islets covered in mangroves at the mouth of the Lostmans River. Two hours after leaving the Hatteras, I idled up to an old pier attached to a condominium complex. I hiked past the condos to S. Collier Street, where I found a mini-mart with a pay phone.

26

Hundred-dollar bills stuffed Armado's wallet until it bulged. I counted them–twenty-two hundred dollars. More than enough to grab a bite to eat and catch a taxi north. He also carried three credit cards. I'd wait to use those, not wanting to be tracked yet. By now, Moralez might realize his son was missing. I was hoping not, preferring to break the news to Moralez myself.

The clerk had no trouble breaking a hundred for a Snapple and a box of dried out chicken tenders that spent more time under the heat lamp than most celebrities. I used the pay phone to call a taxi, which took nearly half an hour to arrive.

The driver balked at taking me all the way back to Englewood, but when I offered him an additional two hundred dollars, he changed his mind. The drive took two hours, and I was feeling like this week had been nothing but trips up and down the west coast of Florida. Everything took forever to drive. Traffic in Florida may be the most miserable aspect of living down here.

"Your car's been robbed," the driver told me when he pulled up behind the Versa with its missing windows.

"Yeah, the neighborhood has gone to shit," I joked as I passed his money over the seat.

While I was gone, an ambitious policeman slapped a sticker on the back of the rental, marking it for impound. I guessed they thought someone stole it, given the condition it was in. It might disappoint the tow truck driver when he arrived to find it gone.

Pay phones in Florida were a rarity, and I'd already hit the jackpot today after finding one. After driving around several blocks, I finally found another next to a taco truck.

I called a local florist, ordering a rush delivery to Moralez's home. The message I attached read "From Armado" and the number for the pay phone. The florist assured me they would deliver the bouquet within the next two hours. While I waited, I ordered some street tacos, opting for the pork and chicken.

The phone rang three hours after I called the flower shop.

"Who is this?" an accented voice demanded over the line.

"Where's Moralez?" I asked, recognizing the voice wasn't the drug lord's.

"Where is Armado?" the voice asked.

"I'm guessing–Gaspar. Right?" I commented.

"Gordon," he hissed. "You didn't get the message the other day, did you?"

"Oh, I got it," I remarked. "Which is why we are here. I want to talk to Moralez."

"*Señor* Moralez is not available," Gaspar stated. "You'll talk to me."

"Then, you tell him Armado will be dead," I snapped, slamming the phone into the cradle. Not that it mattered. The act of slamming a phone down has long since lost its effect. I'm not even sure it was all that clear before everything was digital. The other party never even glimpsed the raw emotion generated toward the receiver. At best, they got a click.

The phone rang again.

"Moralez?" I asked, answering the phone.

"Gordon, you'll talk to me," Gaspar demanded.

"Okay, asshole," I commented. "Let's talk. Right now, Armado is not in a position to survive. I can fix that with a quick call to an agent in the DEA. They can pick him up. Of course, he's sitting on Juan's 250 kilos of coke and a corpse of your good friend, Dominico Berríos. That's all I have to say. Tell Juan he has ten minutes to call me back. Not you. Moralez."

I hung up again.

The timer in my head started as soon as I hung up. Eventually, I planned to do exactly what I told Gaspar, turn Armado over to the Feds. But it didn't need to be just yet. If he didn't call back, I'd need to rethink my strategy.

He called. It was eighteen seconds short of my ten-minute deadline.

The phone rang three times, and I considered leaving it unanswered, but it was too risky. I might have overestimated how much Moralez cared about Armado. He might not call back.

"Hello," I answered on the fifth ring.

"Gordon," Moralez grunted into the phone.

I guessed over the last ten minutes, Moralez attempted to call Armado. Maybe he tried to track his phone, although it seemed stupid for a member of a cartel to use those tracking apps. Personally, I find it stupid to use it when I'm not breaking any laws. My privacy is important. Of course, I don't even own a cellphone, and it wasn't likely I'd be signing up soon.

"You got my message," I commented.

"Where is my son?" he demanded.

"He's safe enough," I remarked. "Where are Velasquez and the girl?"

He grunted something about them being tucked away.

"Here's the deal," I explained. "I have Armado, the coke, and Berríos. Not to mention the gun that your son used to kill him. I tied all of that up nice and neat. It's just waiting for someone to open the gift. It can be you, or it can be the DEA. Those are your options."

"I think you are bluffing," he retorted. "Can you prove you have Armado?"

"You know," I admonished. "How did I know he killed Dominico?"

That tidbit of realization hadn't clicked with him yet. When it did, he let out a brief gasp. "You were on the boat?"

I chose not to answer him. Let the thought stew around in his head. I was close enough to kill him, yet he had no clue. "Berríos," he murmured under his breath, understanding the trap his own man sprang.

"I want Velasquez and Rosalina released now," I insisted.

"They aren't here," he remarked, still somewhat dumbfounded at how close I'd gotten to him. His mind registered the implications. His house, his son, everything was now out there. Privacy is a prerequisite for running an illegal operation like his. Now, even if I didn't have the upper hand, the playing field leveled.

Moralez lived in Englewood, while the video I saw last night showed Scar in a warehouse. I didn't know enough about the Englewood area, but from the houses I saw, there wasn't much of a warehouse district.

"I'll give you two hours to get Velasquez and put him on the phone with me."

He stammered, trying to regain some composure and decide on an appropriate path through this mire I just created. "That's not enough time."

"Two hours," I repeated. "Any past that and I'll gift wrap Armado. He's a little too dainty. How quick will he turn on you?"

The speaker made a muffled sound, as if he covered the microphone to talk to someone else. Finally, he responded, "I'll do what I can."

I hung up the phone. A man like Moralez had contacts. By now, they were searching for Armado. His phone was in the bottom of the Gulf. I checked before disembarking the yacht–the Hatteras didn't have AIS, a vessel identification system for spotting other boats on the water. If there was another tracker on the yacht, I never saw it.

Armado wasn't his only quarry. He'd find someone to trace the number of the pay phone, if he hadn't already done so. I planned to move anyway, but now there was a ticking clock.

"Okay, Gordon," Moralez responded. "Two hours."

Without another word, I hung up the phone. The next call I made was to Jay's cellphone.

"Delp," he answered.

"Jay, it's me."

"Flash," my friend responded with some trepidation. "Everything okay?"

"I'll let you know in a few hours," I told him. "I need a favor. Can you get me a landline for an address in Englewood?"

"Do I want to know?" he asked.

"I'll tell you about it tomorrow over a beer," I offered.

"What's the address?"

I gave him Moralez's street address.

"Can you give me about fifteen minutes?" he asked.

"Yeah, I'll call you back in an hour or two," I told him, leaving him with a vague answer.

"I'm here all day," he quipped.

After hanging up the phone, I drove toward Moralez's house. If I passed Gaspar or any of the guys who visited my motel, they might recognize the Versa. I had few options. Just hope I didn't stand out.

As I turned onto Highway 776, a familiar Lincoln passed me going the opposite direction. I made a U-turn and trailed them, staying eight to ten cars back. The black car continued east onto the Tamiami Trail for another twenty minutes. I dropped back to about twelve cars, trying to stay out of sight. The Lincoln shined like new, making it easy to track without getting too close.

When it pulled off the road, I followed several seconds later. Now there were only two cars between us, and it made me nervous. I pulled into a lot for a janitorial supply company, giving them several seconds to increase their lead. Without too much of a wait, I was back on the road. The brake lights of the Lincoln flickered a quarter of a mile ahead of me. It made a left, and when I reached the same intersection, I saw it turn right.

They were driving through a section of older commercial buildings, built in the early eighties based on the style. When I reached the second street, I was about to turn before I realized they'd pulled into a lot just after the intersection. I drove past, looking for a place to turn around.

By the time I made it back, the Lincoln was empty. I guessed they went inside. There was no place to park and watch the car, so I drove back to the previous intersection, backing in a small alley behind an empty building.

After ten minutes, the Lincoln drove back past me. I couldn't see inside, but I hoped Scar was in there. I considered searching the building where the Lincoln parked, but time was of the essence. If everything didn't go as planned, I could return. A creeping worry oozed through me. What if Moralez just eliminated his hostages, writing off Armado?

The Versa slipped back into traffic, following a quarter mile behind them. I passed the turn when the Lincoln followed 776 toward Moralez's home. Instead, I pulled over at the next gas station I could find with a pay phone.

"Delp," Jay answered.

"You got one?"

"Not even gonna kiss me hello," he retorted in his Mississippi drawl.

"I'm gonna have to owe you," I replied.

He chuckled to himself as if some untold joke amused him. He gave me the number, followed by, "Flash, you better be careful."

"You saw a name to go with that number?"

"I am a fucking detective," he scolded.

"Let's hope I have it all under control," I told him, hoping to assure myself as well as Jay.

"At least I'll know where to look for a crime scene," Jay commented wryly.

"See, there's always a bright side."

He groaned before hanging up on me.

It had been close to two hours. The Lincoln had enough time to reach the house. Moralez would call within the two hours. I was sure of that. He'd cut it as close as he thought he could. Of course, it was a good bet one of his men was watching the pay phone I used earlier. He might worry when I hadn't shown up yet. At exactly two hours, I imagined the phone ringing there. Perhaps some stranger would answer or it would just ring and ring.

Another fifteen minutes passed. In my mind, I thought Moralez might be panicking. I wasn't where I told him. Was he being played? That train of thought would help, but with someone like Juan Moralez, a lack of control like that could lead to rash actions. I wanted to keep him on the line but not give him enough slack to break free.

Fashionably late, I dialed the number Jay gave me. The phone rang twice.

"Hello?" Moralez answered. The uncertainty layered through his voice.

27

"How'd you get this number?" Moralez demanded over the phone.

"C'mon, Juan," I scolded. "I wasn't waiting around for you. I found your house. How hard do you think your phone number would be?"

He seemed to fume silently.

"Do you have Velasquez and Rosalina?" I questioned.

"They don't go free until I see Armado is alive," the drug lord stated.

"This is only going to happen if you do what I tell you," I iterated. "The time for negotiations ended when you sent your lackeys to beat the shit out of me. Now we do things the way I want or I walk."

Moralez seethed through the phone. He wasn't used to be talked to in that manner. Men like Moralez and Moreno often believed in their own hype. They became so accustomed to the respect they received, they forgot it was not actually a gift. Such reverence is always bought. Well, perhaps not always, but usually. It's purchased with fear and intimidation, sometimes supported by financial rewards. I didn't doubt Gaspar or Berríos received a tidy reward, but I had trouble believing even an asshole like Berríos would murder his own son unless something scared him. Sometimes the fear of something else overpowers the requisite respect, like when a pissed off former Marine breaks into their home and tells their wife he's coming for them. It's those moments that test loyalty. Whether it's someone like me or the Feds coming down on them.

Moralez bought into his own hype. He almost shouted into the phone, "Gordon, you don't intimidate me. I'm not doing anything until I see Armado."

I dropped the phone onto the cradle, disconnecting him. If I'd been with Armado, I might use the video to show Moralez what I could do. That wasn't really my style, but Armado didn't need to know that. I could push his fear to a breaking point without actually harming him.

Instead, I bluffed him. Well, mostly it was a feint. I needed this to end as much as Scar did. Preferably with both of us still alive. If this didn't work, I'd still hand Armado over to the Feds. It might not mean Moralez ends up behind bars, but I'll deal with that bridge when I get to it.

I counted out another two minutes before I called him back.

"Don't hang up on me!" he demanded.

"Shut up," I demanded in a calm voice.

"Uh..."

"I want to talk to Velasquez," I told him.

"No deal," Moralez responded, regaining his composure. "I'm done doing this your way."

"Do you want me to hang up and walk away?" I questioned him. "You are going to prove that the two of them are still alive."

The phone was silent for several seconds. I wondered how he was trying to handle this. He wasn't alone. If he gave into me, it displayed a chink in his armor. It was possible Moralez actually understood the type of respect he garnered. How he handled my disrespect could affect how his men viewed him.

"How do I know Armado is alive?" he asked. His tone was gruff, but there was a slight tremor in the way he spoke. If I hadn't been thinking about it, I would have mistaken it for part of his accent.

"You're going to have to trust me," I replied. Despite the impression I wanted him to have, I wasn't holding all the cards. But there was no way to meet his demand. I had to sell him the idea he had no other option. "He is safe for now. I give you my word."

"No, it doesn't work that way, Gordon," Moralez insisted. "What does your word mean?"

"I know you don't know me," I explained. "If you did, you might have left me alone. The thing is, I have a piece of me that's ingrained with the idea of honor. It's what keeps me going. Right now, understand that when I assure you, on my honor, that Armado is safe, I'm telling you the truth.

"It's the way it has to be," I added. "The sooner I speak with Velasquez, the quicker you can get to Armado."

Moralez muttered something in Spanish over the phone. I assumed it wasn't a blessing for my children. A shuffling sound came over the line before I heard Scar.

"Gordon," he addressed me. His voice was scratchy and deeper than usual, as if he could barely garner the strength to talk.

"You're alive?" I asked.

"No shit," he rasped.

"Rosalina? Is she safe?"

"Yeah," he grunted. "Relatively."

"Hang on a bit," I told him.

"Gordon, this is insane," he chided. "Cut us loose."

"Eh, if it was just you, I might," I told him.

He sighed before Moralez took the phone back from him.

"You heard him," he announced. "Where is Armado?"

"Keep him safe," I advised. "I'll call you back with a location."

"Gordon..." he argued, but I disconnected the line.

Now that I confirmed Scar was still alive, I wanted to get back south before I gave Moralez the coordinates of the Hatteras. Since I assumed Moralez would try to trace this number, there wasn't much time to stick around. I drove south, returning to Marco Island.

If I never sat in a car again, I think it would be a relief. This constant back and forth wore on me. Sure, I'd get a little wet bouncing around in my dinghy, but at least I was on the water. Not surrounded by concrete and a thousand other drivers zipping in and out of the surrounding lanes with no cares in the world. Automobiles were the surest way to death and injury. Everyone asks me why I'm not worried about a tragic boat accident. We see the news stories at least once a month about a boat capsizing or two vessels colliding. The thing is, we only remember those tales because of their infrequency. How many people die in an automobile accident every day? I don't know, but it's a lot more than boating accidents. I'd rather take those odds and end up anchored off a sandy beach than tied to a desk in some drab office.

When I reached Marco Island, I found the same phone I'd used earlier to call a taxi, but this time I called Padrino's.

"Padrino's," a young girl answered. I couldn't tell if it was the same one I'd spoken to earlier.

"Hi, I need a favor," I told her.

"Uh..." she stammered.

"First, my name is Chase Gordon. You should ask Julio Moreno if what I ask you to do is okay, before you do it."

"Uh... okay," she responded, confused.

The last thing I wanted was a young hostess to cross Moreno on my account. It was going to be a little bold on my part, and no matter how it ended, someone was going to be on the wrong end of it. With any luck, it wouldn't be me.

"I need you to go out to the van on the street and ask for Agent Kohl. If he's not there, tell whoever is that Chase Gordon needs his phone number."

"The van?" she asked.

"Ask Mr. Moreno," I told her. "I'll call back in a few minutes."

I hung up, worried the girl was more confused than she should be. After fifteen minutes, I called back.

"Padrino's," the girl answered.

"Me again," I told her.

"Hold on," she demanded a second before the canned music sounded.

"Chase?" Moreno asked when he picked up the phone.

"Julio," I acknowledged. "Good. She did what I told her."

"Yes," he responded. "I'm glad you insisted on that. It might have caused a bigger uproar had I not known."

"You're a reasonable man, Julio. I trusted you to understand."

The man sighed into the phone. "I'm not sure I do. What are you doing?"

"Would you believe me if I told you I wasn't sure yet?" I asked. "It's either a game of Three-Card Monte or Hide and Seek."

I envisioned the drug lord shaking his head in confusion when he replied, "I'm not sure I understand."

"Sorry," I admitted. "Those aren't great examples. I'm trying to remove Moralez from the board while saving Esteban."

"And Agent Kohl?" he asked. "How do you plan to employ him?"

"If everything goes according to plan, which means my timing has to be pretty exact, then Kohl gets to be the hero."

"I see," Moreno commented. "Kohl is a tenacious agent. He's been hounding me for years."

"Maybe a win with Juan Moralez will distract him from you."

"Somehow, I doubt it," Moreno bemused.

"Did your hostess get the number?" I asked.

When he read it off to me, Moreno asked, "Are you sure Esteban is still alive?"

"He was a little over an hour ago," I assured the man. "I think I've given Moralez substantial reason to keep him that way—as long as I keep the cards moving."

After hanging up with Moreno, I added talking on a phone to my list of things I was growing tired of this week. If I didn't have to do it again for a while, my ass would be relieved. Instead of bemoaning it, I dialed the number Moreno gave me.

"Kohl," the agent answered.

"This is Chase Gordon," I responded.

"Gordon, dammit. What the hell do you think you are doing? The girl was just a teenager."

"Chill out, Kohl," I insisted. "I didn't think you'd shoot her."

"No, you blew our cover with your Cuban friends," he griped.

"Your cover?" I quipped. "You mean the cable television truck that's been sitting a block from Padrino's for a year? That cover?"

"We change the truck regularly."

"To what? A plumbing truck," I retorted, almost laughing. "Don't be stupid. We both know at this point the surveillance is merely for intimidation. Moreno takes measures to ensure you get nothing worthwhile, and since you probably don't have enough to arrest anyone, you lie in wait, hoping to scare up a low-level informant–if you're lucky."

"Fuck you, Gordon," the agent cursed.

"That's no way to talk to me," I rebuked. "I'm going to give you a present."

"What?" Doubt laced his voice.

"Juan Moralez."

"Is this some half-assed attempt to steer me away from your buddy?" Kohl prodded.

"No, this is an opportunity for you."

"I smell bullshit," the agent expressed.

"Let's say it's not. Suppose I wrapped Juan Moralez and his son up with a dead body and enough cocaine to drop them in prison for several years?"

"How did you do that?" he demanded.

"Not yet," I explained. "You have about two hours to get to Everglades City. You'll need a couple of boats."

"I can't do that in two hours," he insisted.

"I might stretch it to three, but after that, Moralez will be gone."

Kohl groaned. "I'll see what I can do."

"Good, I'll call you back in at least two hours," I assured him. "Make sure your phone stays charged."

"This better not be a waste of time, Gordon," he threatened.

"I hope not," I told him. "This is the best I can do."

I hung up before he could threaten me more. If it fell apart, he might stick a charge on me. Nothing too severe, but enough to cause me problems for a long time.

My next call was to Moralez again.

"Where are you?" he demanded.

"Marco Island," I told him. "Bring Velasquez and the girl here. It's almost six. If you hurry, you can get Armado back before nightfall." That wasn't true. Even if he made it to Marco Island before dark, it was a two-hour dinghy ride to the Hatteras.

"Is Armado there?" Moralez asked.

"Very close." It wasn't a lie. If they had something faster than the little motor on the dinghy I rode in, it would take less than an hour.

"We are on the way," he told me.

"You can bring two guys," I explained. "Gaspar and one other. No more or the deal is off."

"Fine," he growled.

"Give me a cell number where I can reach you," I insisted before he hung up.

28

A Cheshire cat grin loomed from the southeast, reflecting off the black water. The bright lunar light allowed me to see the foamy peaks of the small waves tumbling toward the shore. My back pressed against the plaster wall on the balcony where I sat, waiting for my quarry.

It took a few minutes to decide which condo was empty. I needed a building that was four or five stories above the small dock with a straight-line view of the small boat I drove from Moralez's yacht. The one I found hovered six stories above the dock. Its owners lived somewhere up north, and this escape provided an easy getaway from the chaos of Atlanta, Birmingham, or wherever they ran on their rat wheel.

By now, I'd left Armado tied up in the head for over sixteen hours. I didn't envy his position. Berríos was likely turning a little ripe himself. While Armado should be able to survive that long, I worried he might just give up. I didn't think he actually had the strength to break free. Certainly not the determination. I saw his eyes. Someone was supposed to do it for him.

Despite his age, he wasn't much more than a kid. He never had to land on his own feet because someone was there to catch him. It even made sense he found some perverse pleasure in killing Berríos. It wasn't the first time he murdered some helpless victim. The way he swung around with the .22 was dramatic. He killed him with a flourish—something to show off for good old dad.

If someone dropped Armado into a pit with almost anyone who knew how to fight, the kid would fold. He had no penchant for killing someone who could kill him. People like Armado don't understand the finality of death. He's seen it, sure. Even caused it. But he's never faced it. If I were to guess, being bound in the bathroom of the Hatteras was the scariest moment of his life. If I rode out to the yacht, I'd find him whimpering in the head and blaming someone else for his condition.

I didn't feel sorry for him. At least, not for his current predicament. Any sympathy I felt focused on the life he was born into. With Juan Moralez as a father, his life's path seemed predetermined. His career or personal goals didn't matter. Eventually, Moralez expected Armado to take over what Moralez had built. His entire life forced him to devote himself to that goal. Some people are not malleable enough to mold into another image properly. The result is sometimes grotesque. If Armado Moralez took over for his father, the cost paid in bloodshed would escalate as he continued trying to prove himself.

The gulf breeze blew against my face as I lolled my head back. By my estimation, Moralez should arrive any minute. I wished more than once I'd brought a rifle along. From this nest, it would be an easy three shots to drop Moralez and the two men he brought. Scar and Rosalina could leave here with little worry. I was not half the marksman Jay was, but even from this distance, I could drop all three.

Of course, shooting him might not solve everything. I assumed he had no intention of following my orders. If the roles were reversed, I'd attempt to stack my deck. He'd show up with the two guys I allowed, but there'd be a couple more waiting. Either their job was to grab me before I approached or kill me once I surrendered Armado.

I pulled out the phone I bought at the mini-mart before I scaled my way onto the balcony. It's immensely easier to jimmy open a sliding glass door from a darkened balcony than try to break in through the front door in a lighted hallway. Even the climb wasn't too strenuous. The architect designed the building to fit as many condominiums as possible, and since balconies added value, each unit had its own. There was only a three-foot gap between the railing of each balcony, making climbing from one to another far more simple than it should have been. I was surprised more kids didn't fall to their deaths trying to play Spider-Man up here.

The text message I sent to Moralez told him to go to the dock at this address. I waited for a response, but none came.

My thoughts mulled over what might go wrong. The problem was it was too much. Moralez could just not show up. Or if he did, it might be the whole thing was simply a ruse to draw me out. If he did what I told him, he might insist on taking either Scar or Rosalina as insurance. What if Kohl ignored me? Or just didn't get here in time?

How many guys did Moralez employ? I started counting in my head. Four were dead by my hand, plus at least the two Scar killed at Oxenwise's house. Armado shot Berríos. Those had to be his closest associates. He still had Gaspar, Throat Tattoo, Monkey Face, and the Driver. How many more did he have? Especially men he trusted?

It took Moralez almost twenty minutes to arrive. He was faster than I thought, which hopefully told me enough.

I expected Gaspar and either Throat Tattoo or the Driver to show up with Moralez. I guessed it would be Throat since he needed someone to keep Scar secured. The other two would hang back. They'd arrive in their own vehicle a few minutes before Moralez. Since there was no way to watch the street and the dock, I walked the area around the condominium.

If they parked down the street, I calculated two simple routes to get here while staying in the shadows. One followed behind the apartment complex across the street. There was even a perfect vantage point where one could see all the way down the path leading to the dock. It would be easy to come up behind me if I made my approach that way.

The second route was a worn path from a neighboring condo. Years of kids traipsing through the brush left a single-file dirt path with ample cover. From there, they could come up on the dock with no warning. However, it took me almost fifteen minutes to discover it. The entrance was behind the mini-mart, and an overgrown hibiscus bush obscured the path.

As quickly as Moralez arrived, I gambled they were at the apartment complex.

I was wrong, though. Moralez arrived with Gaspar and Monkey Face. Scar had both of his hands bound behind his back, with something covering his face. They treated him like Hannibal Lecter, taking no chances on him breaking loose. A smart move considering Scar's lethal skillset, coupled with a heavy dose of vengeance.

Once I saw the five of them walk toward the end of the dock, I slipped back into the darkened condominium and exited through the hall. The building had a side entrance leading to a parking lot. When the architect designed the condo, he put the parking area on the opposite side from the walkway. Probably for aesthetics. It didn't block anyone's view, and the vehicles weren't visible from the beach. No one wants to stare at dirty cars when there is sand, surf, and bikinied girls to watch.

I crossed behind the cars, staying between the two aisles. If someone glanced my way, I'd still be hard to spot. Not impossible, though. Sometimes, the best bet is not to slink around. Act like one belongs, and get there fast. The longer someone stands around looking suspicious, the more likely a passerby will spot them.

For the moment, my M45 remained tucked in the back of my shorts. If I could avoid using it, it would be best. Besides the fact that one gunshot would alert Moralez at the dock, it was still early enough in the evening the residents were all still awake. Not only awake, small groups were moving about on the street and beaches. It was a Florida beach town, and there might be an actual ordinance requiring a certain number of walks along the beach when a person visits. Most were couples strolling along to enjoy the gentle breeze and moonlit waters. Others were families, bringing the kids out to chase crabs back into the sea while they giggled. It was enough traffic to prevent me from pulling my weapon too soon. No need to create a panic.

South Collier Boulevard sported enough traffic and pedestrians to allow me to blend in. Once I casually crossed the street, I ran between two buildings to flank the apartment building. I spotted the Driver first. He was leaning against a red Bronco. His skills were limited to driving because, as a surveillance operative, he failed miserably. By following his eyes, I pinpointed Throat Tattoo hunched on the second-floor walkway behind a potted plant.

The inked thug watched the path across the street intently while his partner watched him. If I gave them the benefit of the doubt, the Driver could be waiting on a signal from Throat Tattoo. I figured the Driver was the weakest link, and they left him back to stay out of the way.

I straightened up and strolled toward the Bronco. The thin Latino man turned as he heard me approach. In the dark, he registered a resident walking back to his apartment. By the time he recognized me, the butt of my .45 cracked him across the temple. As he dropped, I caught him under his armpits and dragged him to the back of the truck.

Before I left the balcony, I started counting off the seconds. It took me 126 to get across the street. Another sixty-seven to find and incapacitate the Driver. I wanted to call Moralez within the next three minutes. If I waited too long, he might get nervous and bolt.

I hurried to the northern end of the building and jogged up the stairs. If Throat Tattoo looked back, he might notice the Driver was missing. My feet crept around the walkway until I was around the corner from Throat Tattoo. He would not go as easy as the Driver. However, I owed him a beating.

Since it worked on the Driver, I tried it again. I turned the corner casually and walked toward Throat Tattoo. His eyes remained locked on the dock across the street. No doubt his instructions told him to not let me get close to them. I realized he was holding his phone in his hand, ready to message, when he spotted me. In the shadows, he didn't immediately recognize me. Like anyone lurking in places they shouldn't be, he attempted to blend into the scenery–turning as if he was only out to enjoy the night air.

"Hey man," I called to him. "What are you doing?"

Startled, the muscle-bound figure jerked back around to explain himself to whoever called him out. My fist hit him right on the letter T in the tattoo. He gasped, realizing in that instant who I was. I didn't give him time to take another breath. I thrust my fist into his throat again. My left hand followed it, cracking his nose and throwing his head back.

I swept my left leg behind his ankles, buckling my right knees as I dropped. The metal railing let out a dull clang as the back of his head slammed against it. Dazed, he tried to stand, and I stepped into a sidekick that landed just below his sternum. The force drove him back into the railing, and I twisted completely around to land another punch.

Throat Tattoo teetered over the railing. An almost squishy thud resounded as he slammed into the concrete. I glanced over to see if he was moving. The threat of his getting away was pooling on the sidewalk.

I walked back to the north steps and crossed to the mini-mart. Time was speeding up. It would take only minutes, if that long, for a resident to notice the corpse on the sidewalk. An alarm would go out, and cops would show up. I needed to make the most of those few minutes before all hell broke loose.

As I pushed the hibiscus plant to the side, I realized I'd over shot my time. It had been almost four hundred seconds since I left the balcony. Close to seven minutes.

I pulled the phone out of my pocket and dialed Moralez.

29

"Where is Armado?" Moralez demanded again over the phone.

"He's parked out there somewhere," I told him, crouching in the brush at the end of the path from the mini-mart.

"Bring him to me," Moralez insisted.

"Sorry," I corrected. "See that boat there? It's the tender from your yacht. You head south in it. I'll call you and give you more accurate directions."

I heard him say something to Gaspar in Spanish.

He put the phone back to his ear. "If you don't call me in fifteen minutes, Gaspar is going to drown the girl."

"I'd hurry," I encouraged. "I left him tied up in the bathroom. He's probably a mess now."

He muttered something in Spanish before hanging up. I assumed it wasn't polite. As I watched the man climb into the dinghy, I dialed Kohl's number.

"Kohl," the agent answered.

"It's Gordon," I told him.

"Fuck, Gordon," he cursed into the phone. "You dragged me all the way out into the swamp. What do you want?"

"Juan Moralez is on his way to a Hatteras yacht where his son is. I'd suggest you wait until Moralez gets aboard before you swarm him."

The agent groaned. "Where is this?"

I recited the coordinates to him. "I hope you have enough men."

"Don't you fucking worry, Gordon," he snapped at me.

"Do you have to be so rude all the time?" I questioned.

"What's in this for you?" Kohl asked me.

"I'm just trying to stop an evil man," I replied.

"There better be enough evidence to put them away," he stated.

"As long as you get them before they dump it all."

"You're going to tell me how you came about all this information."

"Sorry, Kohl," I told him. "Consider this an anonymous call."

I hung up and watched as the little motor pushed the tender away from the dock. Moralez took the boat alone, something I didn't expect. It made sense. He assumed I was making a play for Scar and Rosalina. As I made my play, he'd let Throat Tattoo and the Driver slip up behind me.

When the sound of the little motor transformed from a putter to a whisper to nothing, I called Moralez with the same coordinates I gave Kohl.

"I can't do anything with that," the man growled over the motor.

"Just south of Everglades City is a cove. Look at the map on your phone. Go through the Thousand Islands and veer east. If you follow the coastline, you'll see the boat."

"Gordon, if they aren't there, your friends are dead," he threatened. "I'll spare no expense in killing you myself."

"You know that's what started all this," I pointed out before hanging up.

It was in the hands of Kohl and Moralez now to meet up. Mentally, I crossed my fingers, hoping the stars lined up. However, I still had Gaspar and Monkey Face to handle.

I slipped the M45 from my waistband and came up onto the pier's walkway.

The wooden bridge stretched fifty yards from the shore to the end of the dock where the four stood. Monkey Face saw me first, grabbing Rosalina tight. He rested the muzzle of a Browning Hi-Power 9 mm against her temple.

Rosalina belted out a shrill scream. The .45 in my hand leveled at Monkey Face. Gaspar turned and stepped behind Scar. The weapon in his hand wasn't visible, but I figured he had it pressed against Scar's back. If it were me, I'd press the barrel between the sixth and ninth vertebra. If I pulled the trigger, the round would tear through the spine and rip the heart apart.

"Gordon, Mr. Moralez said he'd tell us when to release them," Gaspar called as I continued to step forward.

"Gaspar, you don't have any leverage," I commented in a flat tone. "If you shoot either of them, you lose the only shield you have."

Monkey Face shifted his eyes between me and his partner behind him.

"It won't work, Soldier," Gaspar told me. "Even if you kill us, none of you will get off this dock alive."

My head cocked, and my eyes narrowed on the thug.

"You mean because of your two men across the street?" I asked. "Are they on their way over now?"

Gaspar's eyes betrayed him. Confusion crossed them. He wanted to know how I knew that. Now he wasn't sure what to do. Were his reinforcements on the way? What was he supposed to do now?

"I don't think they are going to make it," I finally told him.

"What?"

"Well, the one with the throat tattoo took a dive off the second floor."

As if on cue, a red light flashed from the street, flooding the pier with bursts of red. Someone must have found him and called an ambulance. If he was still breathing, I had a few more minutes. If not, it wouldn't take long to figure out someone pushed him. I knew the Driver was still alive. In fact, when he woke up, I figured he would make his own getaway. They stuck him in the back for a reason.

Gaspar shook his head in frustration. The thug holding Rosalina had a different countenance. His eyes widened when I mentioned Throat Tattoo. Now, rage was filling them. He wasn't processing all the information fast enough. All that registered in his brain was Throat Tattoo was dead.

In most situations like this, cool and calm heads prevail. There's a reason someone coins a phrase. It's usually true. Of course, these guys panicked. Neither cool nor calm,

Monkey Face whipped the barrel of the Browning toward me, firing wildly.

As he twisted the gun around, I stepped to the right, throwing my shoulder onto the rail as Monkey Face fired with reckless abandon. My body rolled over the top of the railing, plummeting into the surf.

With little time to prepare, I flopped into two feet of cold water. The bottom was a mixture of rocks and sand, leaving me bruised but not too badly bashed. Above me, I heard footsteps running down the dock toward the spot I went over.

Gaspar shouted something in Spanish I couldn't make out. I rolled under the dock as more gunshots peppered the surface.

The .45 came out of the sea as I trained the sights on the wooden planks above my head. I wasn't sure where Rosalina was, but I suspected Monkey Face left her at the end when he ran, without thinking, to shoot at me over the side.

"*¿Dónde estás?*" a voice called as two more shots hit the salt water.

The gunman continued to blast the surface of the water from almost directly above me. He would stand next to the railing in order to shoot at that angle, and I lined up the barrel to where I guessed that was.

"Right here, asshole!" I shouted, leaning forward enough to ensure my voice seemed right below him.

He fired three shots, followed by two shots from my .45.

"Aaah," he screamed, and I squeezed the trigger twice more. "*¡Mi pierna!*"

A large splash sounded at the end, and I jerked around, sweeping the barrel of the gun toward the sound. The moonlight reflected off the foam where someone had struck the water. I sloshed back, raising the weapon in case it was a ploy to coax me out.

"Save him!" a woman shouted, and I found the source–Rosalina.

"It's Esteban!" she cried.

She was pointing toward the surface. Neither Scar nor Gaspar were on the dock with her anymore.

"Where's the other guy?" I called as I caught sight of Monkey Face pulling up on the rail with his left hand.

He lifted the Browning toward me, and I fired twice. The enforcer jerked before falling back onto the dock.

At the end of the dock, a head popped up. Gaspar surfaced, sucking in a breath before submerging again.

I sprinted through the water until I was waist deep. At that point, I dove under the surface, kicking toward the two men. Other than Gaspar coming up the once, neither man surfaced again. Scar was still bound with his hands behind him. He'd struggle to get anywhere without the thug fighting him.

Even with the moon, it was impossible to see anything. My ears popped as I dove deeper. It was at least ten feet deep, but I couldn't tell which way I was going. I kicked to the surface to get my bearings. Rosalina stared down from the railing on the pier.

"Can you see them?" I shouted.

She shook her head. Suddenly, she screamed, raising a finger toward me.

A hand caught me by the shoulder and dragged me under.

Gaspar!

I twisted, jabbing my left elbow back into him. The blows landed softly without fazing the man.

Gaspar pushed up on me, breaking through the water. The gasp of air echoed in my ear. I threw my head back. The back of my skull smashed into his face. The impact shook him loose. I twisted around and slammed the side of my .45 into his face. The man rolled forward, unconscious.

I pushed him over onto his back so he didn't drown right away.

"Do you see him?" I shouted up at Rosalina.

"No," she called.

"Where did he go in?"

She pointed to an area between me and the dock. My head dove as my legs kicked toward the bottom. With zero visibility, I could only feel around. My fingers dug into the sandy muck on the seafloor. I guessed I was about fifteen feet down.

There was no way to tell if I'd searched an area or not. I swam along the bottom for a dozen feet before turning back. As I continued the search for what seemed like an eternity, my lungs ached, begging for oxygen. I kicked a few more feet before turning toward the surface.

My foot dragged across something, and I froze. The water already lifted me off the object. My body rotated toward the bottom again as my feet pushed me down. The first thing I felt was fabric—a shirt.

My hands found his arms and looped under his armpits. Both feet shoved off the bottom, thrusting us to the surface. When my head emerged, I sucked in a desperate gulp of air as I kicked backwards toward the shore. We came up under the dock. The surf pushed Scar toward the shore.

"Rosalina!" I shouted from under the pier. My words echoing against the timbers. "I have him!"

Her response, if there was one, was inaudible in the din of surf bouncing around under the pier. Scar was unconscious and, as far as I could tell, not breathing. When my feet dug into the bottom, I straightened up, dragging the man's bottom out of the water.

"Come on, Scar," I urged him. "Breathe!"

I dropped him on his back at the edge of the water. Sand kicked up as Rosalina ran up to me.

"Is he alive?" she asked desperately.

Without answering, I started chest compressions. My hands pumped his lungs. After years of training, I instinctively stopped at the proper intervals without realizing I was counting to perform mouth-to-mouth.

"Dammit, Scar," I hissed when he still hadn't started breathing.

"The ambulance!" I shouted to Rosalina. "We need help!"

She kicked sand back on us as she bolted for the flashing red lights. In the distance, I heard her voice echoing off the condominium as she cried for help.

After another round of compressions, I gave him mouth-to-mouth again. "Breathe, you fucker," I cursed. "C'mon, Scar."

The man coughed, spitting water up out of his mouth. His chest moved up and down as he hacked more saltwater from his lungs.

"He's over there," Rosalina shouted as she ran up to us with a paramedic.

"Let me in," the medic announced, and I pushed out of the way.

"Is he okay?" Rosalina asked me.

"He's breathing," I replied. "The bastard should be fine."

The girl stared at me. "What about them?" she asked, pointing toward the pier.

"Shit," I cursed, realizing Gaspar was still in the water.

In another circumstance, I had no issue killing the man. But now he was helpless. I couldn't save him and Scar. My feet ran up the dock. I couldn't see him on the surface. The waves may have pushed him under the pier like they did Scar.

A sigh escaped my lips. As I stared at the black water, I realized I dropped my .45 while I was bringing Scar ashore. It wasn't my only one, and by the time the cops dragged the water for Gaspar, they'd find it too.

I walked back to the beach where Rosalina stood watching another paramedic arrive with a stretcher.

"They said he's okay," she told me. "What about that other man?"

I shook my head.

Two police officers came running down the path toward us.

"Rosalina, you have to talk to the cops," I told her.

"What about you?" she asked.

"I bet I'll be in jail until this gets sorted out. Just make sure to stay with Esteban once they clear you. It's important they get the right story."

"He kept trying to protect me," she related. Rosalina stared at the end of the dock. "That man almost killed him because he stopped him from... hurting me."

I nodded. "Then you need to protect yourself now for him. Make sure they know Victor had the drugs, not you."

"Victor?" Her face twisted. "I don't know where he is."

My head shook again. "I'm sorry," I assured her.

"What's going on here?" one officer demanded.

"Officer," I called to him. "These men kidnapped this girl and him. I don't know exactly what was happening, but I shot one of them. The other went into the water with this man. I pulled him out. The other..." I turned to stare at the surf.

"What's your name?" he asked me.

"Chase Gordon."

30

The fluorescent tube buzzed as one lamp flickered. Rust-colored stains peppered the ceiling of the Marco Island jail in abstract shapes. My mind twisted a few into recognizable images. I wasn't sure what caused the odd discoloration. They resembled droplets of liquid that congealed. It did not pique my curiosity enough to investigate more than staring at it from the bunk.

My roommates comprised two twenty-something males still sleeping off the night before. One rolled over an hour ago, vomiting on the floor. Without another sound, he rolled back on to the bed with a glob of puke rolling down his chin.

The officers responding last night weren't used to dealing with the chaos I left on the dock. I expected to spend the night in jail. When I admitted I shot Monkey Face, the cop whose nameplate read, "Stanley," placed me under arrest. He assured me it was temporary until they established what had happened.

Rosalina began spilling out all the details, trying to assure the officers I'd only stepped in to rescue them. Officer Stanley promised her they would sort all the details.

That was the last I saw of Rosalina or Scar. I hadn't even answered a question yet. It was all about wait-and-see.

That seemed to include examining the sludge sprayed on the ceiling.

"Gordon!" a voice announced. "Come on."

"Ugh!" one kid groaned as the officer shouted into the cell.

I rolled off the bunk, dropping to the floor. My feet barely missed the pool of vomit, landing on either side of the puddle.

"Can we go?" the other kid mumbled, however what actually came out of his mouth sounded like, "Cawega?"

"No!" the officer snapped. "Nobody's come to get you boys yet."

The uniformed officer motioned for me to extend my hands, where he cuffed them in front of me. I wasn't being released yet. It was time to face the questions. The officer unlocked the grated door, ushering me out of the communal cell. I tagged along behind him, not asking questions. It was unlikely he had any answers, anyway. His job was little more than babysitting with paperwork. Based on the thickening vomit left by the inebriated kids, it was exactly like babysitting. At least the way I envisioned it. I'd take maneuvering around IEDs over cleaning up children's puke.

The jailer opened a door where two plainclothes detectives sat with a tall, graying man in a tailored suit.

"Mr. Gordon," one detective greeted me. "I'm Detective Cantor. This is Detective Aidan."

"Detectives," I responded, glancing at the expensive suit seated across from them. In the Corps, it was often inadvisable to ask questions when one is expected to have the answer. This had all the earmarks of one of those moments.

If the guy in the suit was associated with the detectives, they would have introduced him. A government employee generally buys off-the-rack. I expected to see Kohl waiting to squeeze details from me, or at the very least, he would torture me with threats of prosecution.

This guy wasn't DEA. He shined like a lawyer with enough spit and polish to hide the grimy exterior.

The fact Cantor and Aidan didn't introduce him meant they expected me to be acquainted with him. I pulled out the chair beside the suit and sat down.

"Mr. Gordon, we would like to ask you some questions," Cantor explained.

I didn't respond. Instead, the suit next to me interjected, "Have you charged Mr. Gordon with any crime?"

Cantor shook his head.

"In that case, I object to his treatment as if he is a criminal," he stated, nodding to the cuffs on my wrists.

Cantor sighed and signaled for Detective Aidan to unlock the restraints. The younger man stretched across the table with a key and freed my hands.

"Mr. Garrett, we would just like some cooperation," Cantor pleaded.

Garrett. I filed the name away. He certainly wasn't my lawyer. I didn't have one. Still, he seemed to help. So far.

I twisted my head to give Garrett a questioning glance.

"Gentlemen, can I have a few moments with my client?" Garrett asked.

The two detectives exchanged frustrated looks before standing up to leave the room.

"We can give you five minutes," Cantor offered, knowing that wasn't true. I could confer with my attorney as long as I needed. However, Garrett simply nodded.

When the door clicked closed, and I was alone with Garrett, he turned to me. "They have nothing substantial to hold you. The girl has already given a statement, saying you saved her. The police haven't found your weapon, either."

I wanted more answers than that. My educated guess told me Garrett was courtesy of Moreno. That didn't mean I trusted him. If anything, it left me wary.

"What do I tell them?" I asked, knowing the answer was always, "As little as possible."

He gave me a story which was edging along the border of the truth. I was in the right place at the right time. It was total bullshit. As I repeated it to the detectives, they knew it was complete bullshit, but it covered the bases. In fact, the tale explained how I saw Monkey Face, whose name I learned was Gomez, kill Throat Tattoo, who the detectives referred to as Alfonzo Ruiz. I tried to stop Gomez, resulting in the shootout on the pier. I also learned that the cops hadn't recovered Gaspar's body, either.

When I finished dumping an entire load of manure on the Marco Island Police Department, Detective Cantor thanked me without a hint of animosity towards me. It was there, but he kept it well hidden.

"Now that my client has answered your questions, I assume he is free to go."

"Yes," Cantor acknowledged. "We will want Mr. Gordon to remain around for a few days."

Garrett shook his head. "Mr. Gordon lives in West Palm Beach. Unless you intend to arrest him, he is free to return home, correct?"

Cantor nodded again, this time it was begrudgingly.

"If you have further questions for my client, you can direct them through me," Garrett informed them.

While I might not have chosen Garrett, it was difficult to deny his skill. Within minutes, the officers returned my personal items. Before I made it out of the police department, Garrett vanished, leaving me only a business card.

Other than what Garrett mentioned, I heard nothing about Scar or Rosalina. I wasn't expecting to, either. If Scar had the opportunity, he'd slip out of the hospital's care and get Rosalina somewhere safe and secluded.

The Versa was no longer where I'd parked it. Given the condition, I figured the police impounded it. I didn't care to venture back to the police; however, I couldn't afford to pay the rental company for a new car. I used the pay phone at the mini-mart and called the police to report the car stolen. It would take them at least twenty-four hours to remember they were the ones who impounded it. By that time, I'd report it to the car rental and let them fight it out–that's what the extra insurance was for.

I called a taxi that carried me to the bus station. Six hours later, I stepped off the bus in West Palm Beach. Technically, I had a bar shift tonight, but I intended to skip it and crawl into my bed after a long shower.

"Yo, Flash," Jay called as I climbed out of the companionway. I'd popped on board *Carina* long enough to grab a change of clothes and a towel. The showers at the Tilly Marina were a short hike over by the marina office.

I glanced up to see Jay coming down the walkway. As he approached, I closed up the cabin doors and waited for him. Jay didn't ask for permission to board. When a man saves your life multiple times, he gets to forgo such nautical protocols.

"Watch the boots," I warned as he stepped with caution into the cockpit.

"You made it back," he remarked. "Did you save the drug dealer?"

I shrugged. "I guess so."

"You are familiar with an Agent Kohl with the DEA?" he asked.

"Yeah," I responded.

"He was the one hounding you about Tristan, right?"

I nodded.

"He's dead," Jay told me.

"What?" I blurted out, shocked.

"Seems he attempted to raid a boat allegedly owned by Juan Moralez. He had a team of four with him. The boat exploded near Everglades City."

"Oh shit," I cursed.

"Chase," he commented, using my name rather than my call sign. "This is bad. Did you have anything to do with it?"

"Dammit. Yeah," I admitted. "I gave him the information about the boat."

Jay shook his head. "I don't know what is going to come of this. How did you know about the boat?"

"Has my name come up yet?" I asked, ignoring the question.

"I don't know," he told me.

"Jay, I didn't set Kohl up," I assured him.

"But Moralez?"

"I just knew where he'd be," I explained, leaving out the fact I'd kidnapped his son.

Jay shook his head again. "Did you do it to help Moreno?"

"Hell no!" I exclaimed. "Moralez had me in his crosshairs. Plus, there was an innocent girl involved, too."

"Innocent?" Jay asked.

"Mostly," I replied. "What about Moralez?"

He shrugged. "I think they are still sifting the wreckage to find out what happened."

"Flash, you need to cut ties with Moreno," he told me.

"There are no ties," I promised. "He's offered me jobs, but I refused every one of them."

"Except the agent investigating him and the leader of a rival cartel are both killed in an incident you arranged," he pointed out.

"Jay!" I exclaimed. "I'd never do that."

"I know that," he consoled. "But it looks bad. Like either you worked for him or you got played."

I held my breath for a second. Could the entire affair be a giant set-up? I didn't think so. At least as far on Scar's part. His concern for Rosalina was genuine. However, Moreno could have used the opportunity to put me in this position. What if it was a humongous ruse? Hell, even Garrett could be a neat little ribbon.

Jay was right. I'd entertained Moreno long enough.

"I didn't do this, and if it comes to it, I'll put Moreno down."

Jay nodded. I leaned back against the cabin, staring across the marina.

31

The lime squirted into the gin and tonic. The carbonated quinine water bubbled to the top of the rocks glass. I dropped the short wedge of citrus with a splash.

Two days ago, I stumbled out of the Marco Island jail. I hadn't seen Jay since he left *Carina* that evening. So far, I'd seen no sign of DEA, FBI, or the police. I wasn't sure if Jay blamed me for Kohl's death. He might, but he also knew my guilt would engross me. It would be easy to tell myself that Kohl knew the deal. He should have prepared better. Of course, how do you plan for an explosion?

No, if Jay blamed me, he was correct. It was my fault. I didn't give Kohl enough information. It didn't fit my plan, because some subconscious thought urged me to protect Scar and Moreno. Instead, my natural distrust of Kohl stemmed from our last encounter. I was trying to protect a friend who got entangled with some dangerous elements, including Julio Moreno.

I compromised my allegiances when I knew my duties. It was like coming out of a haze to realize one was an uncontrollable drunk. It might not have been my rock bottom, but it was a sufficient wake-up call.

The Manta Club was slow tonight, which only gave me time to think–something I was loath to do. Unfortunately, it seemed fated.

Abby grabbed the gin and tonic, along with the bottle of Blue Moon.

"Do you have a glass?" she asked.

Her request jerked me from my musing. "Oh, yeah," I apologized.

"You okay, Chase?"

"Just lost in thought," I assured her. There was no point in dragging anyone into the morose pit I found myself in. Most people tried to offer support, explaining how I did nothing wrong. It was always misguided, and all it resulted in was people making excuses for their mistakes. Those excuses were easier to handle than learning to live with the wrong. Since several men died the other day because of me, the only honorable thing would be to not only accept my culpability, but dwell on it. Otherwise, we continue to repeat these destructive behaviors with the caveat–it is somehow not our responsibility.

"Mr. Gordon," an accented voice erupted behind me.

I turned slowly to face Julio Moreno, grinning like a damned banshee.

"Julio," I responded with no inflection.

The drug lord was standing with Jorge. I wondered where Scar was. Perhaps he was still recovering. Or his actions left him on the outs with Moreno. I didn't inquire.

The business with Scar and Moreno would no longer be my concern.

As if to cement my decision, the man gloated, "It seems I owe you."

My jaw clenched. "No," I insisted. "Anything I did was only for the girl."

"You'll be glad to know that she is safe," he informed me. "Esteban is taking her somewhere to start a new life."

Inside, I seethed. This man viewed the affair as a victory, and I had become his champion.

"Julio," I began, leaning across the bar. "I need you to understand something."

His left eyebrow lifted an eighth of an inch as if to question me.

I explained, "After this moment, I don't want to see you again."

Jorge interjected, "You don't disrespect..."

I cut him off, stating, "Shut up, or I'll drag your ass across this bar."

Even though I handed him his ass the other day, the big tattooed thug bristled at the threat. He raised up, but Moreno's hand rested on his arm, silently staying his guard dog.

"You are unhappy with me," Moreno commented.

"Not at all," I remarked. "You behaved exactly as I should have expected. I'm unhappy with myself."

"Because of Agent Kohl?" he questioned.

I didn't give him an answer. Instead, I reiterated, "We have no relationship. You don't come around here and ask for anything or demand anything. Don't send threats or invitations. I will rebuff them all, and your men will either come back broken or not at all."

"These are bold words," he growled. His demeanor shifted from the grandfatherly man into the killer he hid beneath the surface. A man like Moreno doesn't grow into power without that streak of death buried there.

"Bold doesn't even come close," I retorted. "Cross paths with me again, and I'll burn your empire to the ground."

Jorge came off the stool, and I locked eyes with the man, inviting him to try me. He paused, waiting for Moreno to stop him. No intervention happened, and the brute realized he might have to come at me again. In his mind, he knew he outweighed me, and the odds would be in his favor. However, doubt is a funny thing. Once it shows up, it crops up no matter how hard one tries to keep it at bay. His eyes gave it away. There was a sliver of doubt, but he also wanted to prove the last time was pure luck on my part. He needed to get that bit of himself back.

The delay was enough for Moreno to rethink whatever instinct the little reptilian part of his brain suggested. He weighed my words, realizing now wasn't the time to challenge them.

"Come along, Jorge," he ordered. As he rose, his face contorted back to the old grandfather. "Chase, I hope you remember that I owe you."

The drug lord faded out into the lobby.

"Damn him," I cursed. He wanted to leave with the upper hand. Remind me that the biggest crime boss in Florida owed me a favor. Then wait until I needed to call that in. It was like telling me he was watching my back.

I checked my watch. It was almost nine. I'd made a hundred bucks tonight. Abby might tip me a third of that. Overall, a slow night.

Somewhere in that moment, I decided it was time to leave. Not for the night. But it was time to leave the dock. I needed some time to clear my head. Time to mourn or maybe sulk was a better term. Actually deal with the losses without masking the grief with alcohol and sex. During that time, I could learn to live with my mistakes.

It would take less than a week to get the boat ready. I completed all the projects I needed to do before I left the dock. The only thing I had to do was stock some provisions and fill the fuel and water tanks.

"Hey, Abby, do you mind closing up for me?" I asked? We wouldn't get many more guests, but if I left early, she wouldn't be obligated to tip me out. On a night like tonight, that affected how much money she would take home.

"Sure," she agreed. "You wanna meet at Pat's later?"

"Not tonight," I told her.

With a slow night like tonight, the bar was clean. Abby just had to toss tonight's garnishes and clean any mess she made.

A gentle breeze came from the north along Lake Worth. Twinkling lights on Palm Beach reflected off the lake. That island never seemed to sleep. Even on a Wednesday evening, the sound of music drifted over the water. Most of the boats at anchor had a single light glowing. Somewhere a small engine pushed a dinghy through the dark.

Even with my state of mind, I took a few moments to enjoy the evening. The moonlight reflected off the still water.

The marina was quiet. It didn't get loud until Thursdays, and the noise escalated until Saturday night as the weekenders filled the docks with beer and music. Usually three different Jimmy Buffett songs and one Zac Brown tune echoed across the water at the same time.

I heard the footsteps, but somehow didn't let the noise alarm me. The chuckle, however, stopped me in my tracks.

"Soldier Boy, Soldier Boy," Gaspar hissed in the dark. He was behind me. I guessed he was waiting in the alcove leading to the maintenance office.

I turned slowly to make out the man's shadow. The LED light behind him offered only his silhouette.

"Guess that's what I get for not letting you drown," I remarked.

"Seems you deserve a great deal," another voice commented from behind me.

My head swiveled to see Juan Moralez standing next to a SeaRay belonging to a dentist in Lakeland.

"I heard you might be dead too," I told him.

"It takes more than an obvious trap to kill me," he snapped back.

"Armado?" I asked.

"You left him to die," he stated, although I didn't believe him. Unless he never intended to save him.

"My condolences," I offered.

The old man took two long strides and hit me in the mouth. The blow knocked my head back. Had the man been twenty years younger, it would have knocked most men down.

"I want nothing from you," he growled.

My tongue ran over my lip, tasting a drop of blood. "Let me guess. This is pure revenge?" I asked.

He motioned his head from side to side. "A little pleasure. A little business," he told me.

Gaspar moved closer, and I recognized the shape of a .45. For a split second, I wondered if it was mine. Gaspar could have recovered it when I dropped it during our struggle. I was relieved to find it wasn't mine, as if the shame of being shot by one's own gun was too much.

"Move," Gaspar ordered, gesturing for me to follow Moralez.

"Where are we going?"

"You have a boat, no?" Moralez asked.

I didn't respond.

"We're going to sink your boat," Moralez told me. "I suppose that part is revenge." He let a chuckle float across the water.

I might have pointed out that it wasn't me who blew up his boat, although he might figure it was my fault the cards landed as they did.

It seemed fitting. Karma sneaking up to pay me back for Kohl–possibly even Kaci and Allie too, along with more than I cared to consider. Many men would consider it recompense. End their suffering so they never had to see those faces of the dead in the night.

But it's a cheap cost. There's no true justice in it. The abacus doesn't work that way. The scales of justice don't actually balance. No, the dead are just forgotten. Not by those who loved them, but by those who could use their memories to level the scales.

I had no intention of dying here. Not tonight, and not because I didn't deserve it.

I never knew Kohl well. He struck me as an asshole, but sometimes tilting against windmills does that to a man. I'd like to imagine if he knew he was sacrificing himself, taking a murderous criminal like Juan Moralez with him would console him.

These boys came at me on my turf. I'd stumbled across the docks in a drunken stupor, and I knew every inch between the Manta and *Carina*, including the missing bolt on the next walkway.

Randy put in a work order a month ago. It was a twenty minute job, but the diver he normally used hadn't made it around yet. It wasn't hazardous, per se. That section rocked farther than the rest, dipping forward at the top right corner. As long as the section remained balanced, there was a slight tilt, but nothing more.

Randy had put up a sign forbidding any golf carts on this dock for fear the weight might snap one of the other bolts. However, the two-inch thick post wasn't in danger of breaking under our collective mass.

But as Moralez stepped past the center, the section tilted a few inches. I made my next stride toward the right, putting all 175-ish pounds on that foot. The corner dropped, sending the back corner up suddenly.

It wasn't significant enough to catapult Gaspar into the water, but he stumbled. I was ready. My right foot pivoted, and my left came up in a quick sidekick. The sudden snap caught the gunman in his abdomen.

I gambled the man wouldn't fire errant rounds at his boss. It's the mistake most people make. If you have a gun in your hand, be ready to shoot it.

Gaspar fell back, and I came around, driving the heel of my right foot toward his head. I might have caught him off guard with the kick, but he recovered, rolling away from me. He didn't have time to raise his gun, but he swiped his right leg at mine with a sweeping motion. I leapt back, avoiding the kick but putting more distance between us. He sprung to his feet as I charged him.

His .45 came up, and I caught his wrist, pushing it back. The two of us toppled off the dock.

The water was black. I didn't focus on the déjà vu of grappling with Gaspar underwater. Instead, my fingers shifted over the top of the gun. I would not lose this one in the dark.

Gaspar struggled, clawing at my face. My other hand jammed up with four fingers under his chin. The blow snapped his jaw together, and if I was lucky, he bit his tongue off. That was unlikely, but it stunned him for a second.

My legs wrapped around his torso. With a wrench, I twisted him around. He lost his grip on the .45, and I tightened mine around it. My free arm snaked around his neck as he attempted to slap at my forearm. The elbow tightened as I jerked his head and neck around.

The crack echoed under water, and Gaspar sank.

I did not know which way I was facing. The black water was the same all around me. My arms stroked a random direction.

Either Moralez ran away or he waited, perched on the dock with a gun, waiting to see who surfaced first. I covered a dozen feet before I drifted to the surface. Once the struggle with Gaspar ended, I tried not to let out a single bubble of air.

My head broke the surface. Only the top came up. My lungs begged for a breath, but I turned slowly instead.

Moralez stood fifteen feet away. He swept what appeared to be a Ruger over the water where Gaspar and I went down. Only now I was behind him.

The barrel of the .45 came out of the water.

"Juan!" I shouted.

The old man spun, firing wildly into the darkness.

My gun jerked a millimeter as I fired one round. Juan Moralez fell back onto the dock as I sucked in a fresh breath.

Also By Douglas Pratt

For a list of books and series by Douglas Pratt
visit www.douglas-pratt.com
or scan the QR code.

Made in the USA
Middletown, DE
22 December 2024